VEXING
THE
HIGHLANDER

TERRY SPEAR

Discover more about Terry Spear at:
http://www.terryspear.com/

ISBN-13: 978-1633110229
ISBN-10: 1633110222

DEDICATION

To my dear next-door neighbor and friend, Carrie Pringle, who has had too many surgeries to count, including brain surgery, came back after her heart stopped three times, and still keeps moving forward. She loves to fall in love with the Highlanders of old and as soon as we met, she fell in love with my world. Thanks for being such a good friend and neighbor!

.

ACKNOWLEDGMENTS

Thanks to Donna Fournier, Dottie Jones, and Vonda Sinclair for being my beta readers and helping to make it the best it could be!

CHAPTER 1

Alban of the Clan Daziel had one mission in mind when his eldest brother, Ronan, the clan chief, ordered him and their brother, Ward, to attend King Malcolm's court—stay out of the king and his courtiers' way. As much as he could possibly manage. Ten guardsmen rode with them to see that they arrived safely and returned in the same way.

Heather and thistle bloomed all across the verdant green glen and rolling hills in waves of light and dark purples and for the moment, it wasn't raining as they rode with their guard force to see the king.

"'Tis time you went to court to see the king," Ward said, but Alban would rather fight Ronan's battles than the king's. Without doubt, he didn't want to attend the festivities at court. Many of those in the Highlands still did not feel they owed allegiance to the king. Not when he had given his eldest son, Duncan, to the English King

William as hostage, and accepted the overlordship of the English king.

"Will he no' be angered that Ronan didna come in my place? I have heard Malcolm has gone to battle for being slighted in the past." Alban was the youngest brother, the shortest, at six-one, yet he still was tall enough to gain attention. His older brothers teased him for being their little brother, though he took their jesting in stride.

"Ronan couldna leave with Sorcha giving birth so soon. Unless our castle was under attack, he wouldna have left for any reason. Certainly not to attend the king's festivities."

"If only we were so lucky to find such a lass." Alban spied more horses up ahead up on the road. "More attendees, it appears. Mayhap the king willna even know if we dinna show."

"We would be missed. Someone is sure to make note of who has arrived and who has no'."

Alban looked out on the lands dotted with stone shielings and stone dykes, ponds, streams, and lochs throughout the area. The sky was bright blue, billowing white clouds casting shadows over the land at one place, then gliding with the windblown clouds across the landscape. "At least we will be staying in tents outside the castle walls. Except for attending feasts, I plan to make myself scarce."

His dark-haired brother glanced at him, his dark eyes smiling. "Aye. As long as you make appearances when necessary. Beyond that, just stay out of trouble. No fighting. Dinna drink too much. Just be on your best behavior. And remember, just be careful about what you say or do while we are there. To earn the good favor of the king, for a coin or two, servants and courtiers alike will serve as his spies in a court. Gossip runs rampant among the servants. Just dinna do anything that will reflect badly on our clan."

"As if I would," Alban said. "Besides, we have some of the same thing at home."

"Only 'tis different because Ronan would believe us before he would anyone else. The king? His loyal staff would probably be believed before Highlanders not completely under his rule would be."

Beside one of the blue lochs, a group of ladies were sitting on blankets and eating, a complement of guards standing around the area watching over them, their horses tied to trees nearby.

Alban and Ward bowed their heads to the women as they approached along the road.

"Courtiers?" Alban asked his brother.

"Or some of those attending court, just visitors like us. The golden-haired woman in the blue kirtle appeals to me. What about you?"

Alban took a longer look at the women, about to say none of them did because he couldn't imagine marrying a woman of the court, or of noble status. Not that he had the chance to, given his position. Several of the lassies were smiling at him, one even bold enough to wave.

Then they all giggled.

Alban smiled, then laughed. "They appeal, though I wouldna wish any of them for a bride."

Ward shook his head. "You willna be saying so if one of the lasses smiles sweetly at you and is quite agreeable."

Alban didn't think it was the case, if she were a lady and ineligible to marry. Wouldn't that just whet his appetite for that which he could not have?

Before long, they reached sight of the massive stone castle. Ward told their men to set up camp in a clearing where no one had claimed the area yet. Tents were already set up all over the glen, different clans having claimed their own temporary spot of land.

"We will see the king's steward and let him know we have arrived." Ward led Alban toward the inner baily where a man was writing on parchment and they both dismounted to speak to him.

"I am Frederick Gustafson, steward to the king, and you are?"

"Ward and Alban, brothers to Chief Ronan of the Clan Daziel, and we will be representing him here."

"He is ill?" the dark-haired steward asked, his brow arched in question.

"His wife is having a bairn. He will be here as soon as he can."

The steward frowned at the notion the chief's wife was more important than the king's business, then jotted down notes.

Alban glanced at his brother, but Ward was frowning at the steward.

"The king has commanded that you stay at the castle. Your men can camp beyond the walls."

"But—" Alban said, not wanting to be confined to the castle. He was sure to speak his mind at some time or another and if he did so, he wanted to do it in front of only Ward so he didn't get himself in trouble. He assumed staying out in the glen, he could speak privately with Ward and get whatever he needed off his chest without being overheard.

"We are honored." Ward gave Alban a dark look, which meant he should be grateful for the king's generosity and not argue with his steward.

The steward snapped his fingers and a lad standing nearby came running. Another immediately took Alban's and Ward's horses and led them to the stable.

"Take these men to the blue chamber," Lord Gustafson said.

"Aye, my laird." The sandy-haired boy was about nine and bowed to them before leading them into the castle.

"Your name?" Alban asked him.

"Tomas, my laird."

"Well, Tomas, do you know what the blue room's importance is?"

The boy's eyes widened and he shook his head. "Nay, my laird. 'Tis just a room for important lairds like yourselves."

Servants were rushing back and forth down the corridor, preparing for the guests' arrivals while Alban wished they were well away from this place. He didn't like that they'd been asked to stay here. That meant the king had to want some concession from Ronan and their people.

"Here 'tis, my lairds." Tomas opened the door to the small chamber. Then he rushed off and left them alone.

The chamber was furnished with one large bed, pegs on the wall, a table, two chairs, and a chest. Alban looked out of the window and saw the tents dotting the countryside.

Smiling, Ward sat on the bed. "No' bad. No' bad at all."

"I agree, except…"—Alban shut the door—"I wonder just why we are here."

Ward left the bed and joined Alban, and the two of them peered out the window. "We can see our clansmen over there." In a whisper, he said, "Remember, everything you say can easily be monitored here. If the chamber is for guests, we may have eyes watching all we do and say. So be very careful."

"Which is just why I preferred staying with our men."

"Even out there, you have to be careful of what you say. No telling who might be lurking about, waiting to hear some bit of gossip to pass along to the king."

"Since we have no choice, do you want me to return to our men and tell them we are obligated to stay here?"

Alban was eager to do so, to get away from here forthwith.

"Aye, but dinna tarry down there. We need to be here in case we are summoned for an audience."

"You mean if you are. You represent Ronan in his absence, not me." And Alban was glad for it.

"No matter. Return as soon as you give word to our men."

"Aye." But Alban fully intended to take his time before he returned. Their brother was laird, and good at leading the men. Not that Alban couldn't do so in battle, but he much preferred leaving politics to Ronan.

Alban stalked across the floor, jerked the door open, and hurried into the hall, eager to leave the place. He was in such a rush to exit the chamber, when he bolted out of the room and slammed the door shut, he ran into a maid carrying a pitcher of water. He barely caught hold of her arm and the pitcher of water before it hit the floor and shattered into a million pieces of earthenware or she fell to join it. The brown-eyed, redheaded wench cried out when he startled her half to death. The pitcher managed to splash water all over them, soaking the front of her brown kirtle and his brat and tunic.

Good thing she wasn't a lady or the news would carry to the king about what a buffoon their new guest was.

The woman was beautiful though, and he stood there with his mouth agape, staring at her creamy skin and flushed cheeks. Alarmingly beautiful. Only she and he were both sopping wet too.

"Beg pardon," he apologized to the woman finally. He'd never seen such a bonny lass before, except for the one he had chased around the loch when he was but a lad, but she was now married to their blacksmith. Well, and Ronan's own lovely wife, and their sister too. But that wasn't the same.

He shifted his gaze from her kirtle where the wet wool clung to her breasts. He hoped she had not caught him gawking at her pebbled nipples, but he had only looked down to see how much of a mess he'd made, not for any other intent.

She looked completely rattled. Could he blame her? "Here, let me refill the pitcher for you."

Her light brown eyes widened, but she managed a small smile. "You are no' wet enough already?"

He smiled back. "I dinna intend to spill anymore."

"Thank you kindly, my lord. But I can manage." She took the pitcher from him and hurried off. She headed toward another room, knocked, glanced at him and smiled to see him watching her with utter fascination. Then the door opened and she went inside and the door shut behind her.

He wished he'd asked the servant's name. He should have told her he wasn't a lord. Brother to one, aye. But that didn't make any difference where he was concerned.

***

Lady Aila couldn't believe what had just happened with the spilled water between her and the Highlander as she rejoined her sister in the chamber. He was gorgeous with his long, dark curly hair, and his dark brown eyes that had melted her right to the spot as she so clumsily ran into him. But she'd been in a rush to fetch the water so she and her sister could wash off the mud from their travels, and he had been in just as much of a rush when he left his chamber too.

She could still feel the strength and warmth of his touch as he'd held her up, making sure she hadn't fallen.

"What in the world happened to you?" Lady Wynda, her older sister asked, her dark hair hidden beneath a veil of pale blue silk. The king had already married her off to one of his barons, but he'd died in battle while serving him. So now Wynda was again the king's ward. The king was eager to marry them both off this time because of their holdings in Scotland, a way to reward his loyal subjects.

In truth, King Malcolm had planned the festivities with that in mind, but they were not the only ones he had brought to court with the same notion. The more alliances he could make with the lords in the area, the better for him when he needed to battle with the English or other Scottish lords who felt they should have been the next in line for the Scottish crown.

"I ran into one of the lords staying in a nearby chamber. Quite literally. He apologized, but my, how braw he was," Aila said to her sister.

TERRY SPEAR

She hoped she would end up with a kind lord, one who would make her pulse quicken, and would intrigue her like the men she'd met whom she never could marry. Not when they had no title and the king would most definitely not have approved. Someone like the Highlander who'd bumped into her and was so gallant about offering to refill her water pitcher.

"I do hope you apologized to him," Wynda said, staring at Aila's gown. "As wet as your bodice is, you need to change. Well, you do anyway, but you need to get the water so we can wash up if you dinna want me to do it."

"Nay, I'll do it."

"You canna go out like that." Wynda motioned to her gown. "What would possible suitors think? That you had wetted your gown to catch their eye, that is what."

Not that it hadn't happened before. Mostly not on purpose—a sudden rain shower drenching the both of them, a boat, several had been crossing a river in, capsizing during rough weather, half drowning them. Or on purpose, but not to catch men's eyes, like when she and her sister had splashed water on each other to cool down on one of those unseasonably hot days, and thought the men watching them were just amused to see the lasses playing in the loch. Until their mother warned them otherwise.

But there was the time that both Aila and Wynda dampened their gowns for the sole purpose of catching lords' eyes. By the time they had found the ones they

10

were half interested in, their gowns had quite dried out.

This was not the same. Rather innocent. And utterly enthralling. Because she did catch the lord's attention, his gaze taking in her breasts, which made the tips tingle in response, and set off a curious little quiver deep in her belly. And lower.

Wynda was now looking out the window at all the tents being set up. "You did apologize to the gentleman, did you no'? If he is as braw as you say."

No, she hadn't. Not because she thought it was his fault, they both had collided with one another at the same time—but because she had been so taken with the gentleman's physique—she'd just stood there awestruck staring at him. What if he already had a wife?

Aila sighed.

"Are you positive you dinna want me to get the water this time?" Wynda, being a dark-haired beauty, appealed to men more than Aila did with her cursed red hair.

Not that she didn't love her hair, but just that most men she had met didn't. "Nay, I will get it. The lord was leaving, so I shall not run into him again." Though Aila wished it with all her heart. She couldn't help that she was such a romantic. Her mother and father had loved one another, and she wanted what they'd had. Though she knew arranged marriages rarely resulted in such a thing. Certainly, it hadn't been so in Wynda and her deceased husband's case. Wynda was more circumspect about this business, having been through it once already.

Aila couldn't help but dream her fate would be better than that.

Both their maids had gotten sick off something they had eaten on the journey here and were sleeping on pallets nearby, or they would have gotten the water for the sisters.

Aila fanned her bodice, glancing down to see if it had dried a bit. She didn't want to change into clean clothes when she was dirty from traveling.

Her gown was still damp, but if she held the pitcher up, no one would notice. She poured what was left of the water into a basin.

Wynda shook her head. "Do hurry though, Aila. We need to be in the great hall for the meal soon."

"Aye, I will fetch it as quick as a mouse. No one will ever notice me." Except if she could catch his eye...the Highlander that was, and maybe she could even learn his name and offer her own.

She hurried down the curved stone stairs until she reached the main floor and saw the Highlander speaking to a lad, Tomas, she thought his name was. She knew it would be unseemly to race across the bailey to the well, just so she could snag the lord's attention. What if she tripped, fell, and broke the pitcher?

So she strode to the well, her gaze on the Highlander the whole time, hoping to catch his eye. Maybe he would again offer to carry water up to her chamber for her. She decided she would say yes this time, and thank him, and apologize to him also.

But the Highlander headed off for the gates, never seeing her. Aila sighed, hoping she could catch his attention later, though with this many people here, she was afraid she would not. Still, if she could, it would be after she had washed up and was wearing a pretty kirtle. A clean kirtle. Not one for wearing while riding on the muddy roads. With horror, she realized what a sight she must be. Did the lord even know she was a lady? Or did he believe she was a servant?

She groaned, quickly filled her pitcher, and hurried back to the chamber.

***

Later that afternoon, Alban and his brother went to the feast and found seats at one of the tables furthest from the head table. Alban was glad for that. Though he was still aware that anything he said, no matter where he was, could be misconstrued and shared with the king.

He kept watching the servants coming and going as they brought dishes to the table, though he was sure the redheaded lass wasn't a kitchen servant.

"Are you looking for anyone in particular?" Ward sounded amused, like he thought Alban had become interested in a servant.

Which Alban had, but he wasn't about to discuss it.

"Here you are more interested with the wait staff, when a lady truly seems to be intrigued with you." Ward raised his brows as if to ask how in the world Alban had managed to captivate the attention of a lady at the king's court when Alban had done no such thing.

At least that he was aware of. Maybe it was the lassie who had waved at them from the loch. He looked around, but didn't see any woman openly watching him. "Which one? There are many, but no one who seems particularly aware I exist."

"The lady over there. She is concentrating on her meal now, blushing to the heavens and back. The one with the pretty red hair."

Alban turned quickly to see the woman, instantly wondering if it was the lass he'd run into, who had been carrying the pitcher of water that had drenched them both. It was she, only now she was wearing a dark blue gown, her hair half hidden beneath veils of silk. "A lady. Are you sure?" Yet the fact she was seated at one of the tables, not waiting on others, and was dressed so fine, ensured him his brother had to be correct. Alban was at once sorely disappointed, wanting nothing more than to see the woman again, but not if her family was titled. He couldn't. He wasn't worthy of her hand in marriage—not based on his position in society, anyway.

He let out his breath and said, "Figures."

But worse, she lifted her gaze and saw him watching her and gave him a bewitching smile, to which Ward said, "Well, well. What have you been up to, little brother?"

And here Alban thought he'd been above reproach the few hours he'd been here so far.

CHAPTER 2

Wynda studied the man Aila was ogling, way too blatantly. Of course when the one sitting next to him had caught Aila's eye while she was trying to catch the other gentleman's attention, she had looked away. But then she saw him talking to the other man and she had been thrilled, and embarrassed to think he might be telling him of her interest in him.

"Is…that the man you had the unfortunate accident with?" Wynda asked, as she finished her fish stew.

"Aye, the shorter one, though he is very tall."

"They must be close friends or related. You have garnered both men's attention now." Wynda tore off a piece of bread.

Aila sipped from her mead and set the tankard down on the table. "He is pleasing to the eye, is he no'?"

"Aye. But is he married?"

That, Aila still didn't know.

Wynda lifted her tankard. "I will ask the king's steward then—"

"Heavens, no. That would show I have interest in him and mayhap he is an incorrigible rake…or worse," Aila said.

"If you are interested in him, what is the harm in learning more about him?"

Aila nodded. "All right. But dinna say *I* am interested in him."

Wynda smiled. "What if the steward were to think I was the one who was intrigued with the gentleman?"

"Just say a distant cousin was inquiring."

"Who isna here."

Aila finished her stew. "Aye."

"Dinna get your hopes up."

Aila's sister had told her time and again that the king would decide this for them when their parents had died and that meant he would want the best alliances out of the proposal. He was not one to consider the lady's fancy.

"He is braw," Wynda said, smiling at him. "I would not toss him from my bed."

Aila laughed. She had never heard her sister speak in such a way about a man. Her husband had been much older than her, gray whiskers and a thinning hairline. Aila had never asked the details of their bed play, nor had Wynda ever breathed a word of it, but in the two years they'd been married, Wynda had never been with child. Had she wanted to toss *him* from her bed?

The meal concluded and everyone waited for the king and his lovely queen, Margaret, and the rest of those seated at the head table to leave before they left the great hall. "Do you wish to hang back and speak with the gentleman?"

"Aye." But when she looked back to see if he might head in her direction, she realized he and the other gentleman had already left. "They are gone."

"Truly?" Wynda looked for them too, but she didn't see either of them. "Well, that is odd. Maybe he is afraid you will spill something else on him." She smiled and Aila knew her sister was not serious, and was, in fact, trying to make light of the men's disappearance so she wouldn't feel bad.

But she just sighed, thinking that he was probably married, or otherwise ineligible. Perhaps he was promised to another, and his being nice to her in the hall was just because he was a kindly lord.

"Come, we must get ready to dance at the festivities once they clear the trestle tables out of the great hall. Mayhap you will see him then and he will ask you to dance."

"Aye, then dinna inquire about him. He may no' be interested in me except as a curiosity."

Wynda touched her hair. "You have beautiful hair."

"So you say." But no one had ever wished Aila's hand in marriage. Even her da had to protect her from mean-hearted men, one who had attacked her for having red hair, saying she was wanton. Her father had beaten him within an inch of his life, even though he'd never been a violent man, save when he had to fight in battles to protect his family and his people.

So she worried that the king would force a man to marry her for her properties, and he would despise her for her red hair. What if she bore him redheaded children? Even worse.

***

Later that evening, everyone was in high spirits as men and women danced in the great hall, while the servants who were not needed were dancing with each other in the inner baily.

Alban folded his arms as he watched the ladies and lords dance.

"You know you can ask her to dance anyway. The king requested our presence, and though you are no' eligible to marry the lass, you are no' a servant," Ward reminded him. He let out his breath on a heavy sigh. "Lady Aila has not once been asked to dance. Be a Highlander, show her a good time. Her sister is very popular. It must vex the younger one that no one seems to be interested in her."

"All right. I will. But it doesna mean she will wish to even speak to me once she learns I am no' a lord."

"You will never know unless you approach her."

"Aye." Alban had been dying to ask her to dance with him the whole time. He couldn't take his eyes off her as she talked away to a couple of eligible maids and her sister when she wasn't dancing.

She didn't seem upset that she was still standing there, though he'd seen her catch his eye once, and she had quickly looked away. Had she already known he was not titled?

Though he was popular with the ladies of his brother's court, he'd been turned down a time or two, so he was expecting the same here.

When he approached, the ladies were all eyeing him, wondering who he was, but all he cared about was Lady Aila. He was gracious enough to acknowledge the other women, then bowed to Lady Aila. "Could I have the honor of dancing with you?"

Her eyes widened a bit and he was surprised she seemed shocked that he would ask. Probably because he had no rank at all.

She curtseyed. "Aye." And with the ladies, who were standing around her, all deathly quiet, he took Lady Aila out to dance.

"I'm no' here to wed any lass," he said quickly.

She smiled up at him. "I wish the same as you, but alas, I dinna believe the king feels the way I do. I thought I might see you after the meal. But you must have left before I had a chance to at least apologize for spilling the water on you."

"I didna know you were a lady."

She paused and stared at him. "You are no' titled?"

"Nay. 'Tis my brother Ronan who is. But his wife is having a bairn and he is yet at home with her. My brother Ward and I are here in his stead. We are with the

19

Clan Daziel. I have never cared anything about titles, happy to be my brother's third in command. I must admit when I learned you were a lady, I wished I was a duke and could court you like any titled lord might."

Her eyes filled with tears and she quickly looked at the floor.

He couldn't believe he'd brought her to tears. "I am sorry, my lady. Allow me to return you to your friends."

"Nay, unless you dinna wish to dance with me."

"You are the only one I wished to. And you need no' apologize about earlier. I was the one who was completely at fault."

She smiled. "No' even my da would admit he was ever at fault with my mother, even when we all knew it."

"I have no trouble admitting I am in the wrong, when I am."

When they finished the dance, he did not leave Aila with her friends, but rather continued to stand by her, not liking that no other man offered to dance with her. He knew if he asked her again, it would show his interest even when he should not. But blast it all, no one was dancing with the lady anyway, so why should she have to stand on the side like this?

"If you dinna think it too presumptuous, would you care to dance with me again?"

She smiled so brightly at him, he was glad to have cheered her. "No one has asked me before."

"They are all buffoons."

Lord Comyn, a blond-haired, blue-eyed earl,

frowned deeply at him, and Alban realized he had done what he was trying so hard not to do, cause trouble for their clan. Yet he wished he could take the lass home with him and prove to her just what he thought of her, how much he genuinely liked her—the way she was sweet and innocent, yet daring enough to dance with him again. And time and again, he'd seen the way she'd looked at him across the tables at the meal, showing interest in meeting him. If it hadn't been for his not having a title.

He'd seen his brother watching him. Now with his arms folded, he looked stern, not angry with him, not concerned exactly, just...watchful. Was he afraid of what kind of trouble Alban might cause them? Possibly. Alban had seen Lady Wynda, Aila's sister, also watching them when she wasn't dancing. Or sometimes even when she was. Was she concerned for her sister's welfare, hoping he wouldn't hurt Aila's chances with a titled lord?

He knew better. The king would decide and neither the lord, if he wished to remain titled, or the lady, would have a say in it. He knew it wasn't any of his concern. That he would return to helping run the clan's lands and fight their battles and leave the king to fight his own, which included making his own alliances, through any means he desired.

After the third dance with the lady, he heard the whisperings. He'd really upset protocol. He saw then the king's steward talking to Lord Dunlap, who bowed, and headed with the steward to join Alban and the lady. He hated that the steward had forced someone to dance with the lady, just so Alban would no longer take a turn with her. When the earl should have been eager to do so without any coaxing.

"If I wouldna create more of a scene than I already have, I would retire to my chamber, satisfied that I had enjoyed the festivities, thanks to you," Lady Aila said.

Alban bowed his head slightly to her. "My lady, the pleasure was all mine." And he meant every word of it. When he returned from his trip here, all he would be able to think of was the beautiful redheaded lass who had stolen his attention. Every redheaded lass would now catch his eye, and disappoint him that she was not Lady Aila.

When she went to dance with the Earl of Dunlap, the king's steward said, "She understands she canna marry you, aye?"

"Aye. No one would ask the lady to dance, and so I did. I hope there is nothing wrong in that."

Lord Gustafson shook his head. "As long as the king doesna disapprove."

"You spoke with him?"

"Aye. He said as long as you encourage titled lords to dance with her, he sees naught that is wrong with it." The king's steward turned his attention from Lady Aila to Alban. "But I will warn you that if you take this too far..." He shrugged. "I shouldna have to tell you what the king does when he isna pleased with one of his subjects."

As soon as the king's steward left, Ward joined

Alban and he figured he might get a lecture. "Ronan will have words with me when he hears what I have done." Though Alban wouldn't have done anything differently.

"Nonsense. Ronan would think these lords too blind to see what a beautiful lady she is. What did Gustafson say to you?"

"Just to leave well enough alone insofar as having anything further to do with the lady. But as far as the dancing went, the king didna disapprove."

"Good. If you have had your fill of the men and women here, let us enjoy the festivities with our own men outside for a while."

"Aye." But Alban had to make a monumental effort to tear his gaze away from Aila as yet another lord was encouraged to dance with her. "Did you dance with anyone?" He realized he hadn't seen his older brother do anything but watch out for Alban's welfare.

"I will. Outside. Less trouble that way. I wouldna have been brave enough to ask a lady to dance. Only you would be so bold."

"I dinna believe I was so bold, but when no one asked her..."

"And you had already shown an interest in her."

Feeling morose about the prospect that Aila would end up marrying some despicable lord she didn't care anything about who didn't care for her either, Alban walked outside with Ward to join in the revelry in the bailey. Though his brother danced with several lasses, Alban had already danced with the only lady he wished to. Still, one of the maids grabbed his hand and pulled him to join the other dancing couples. He was half-enjoying himself, despite his concern for Aila, when he saw her standing near the doors to the keep with her sister watching him.

He lost his place in the country dance and Aila laughed. She didn't appear upset with him for dancing with others, and he appreciated it. He knew he shouldn't ask, but he joined Lady Aila and her sister and invited them to dance with them.

"If we were not at the king's court, we would gladly do so," Lady Wynda said.

Aila smiled. "Aye, we would."

"We are retiring to our chamber, but Aila wished to speak with you before we left." Lady Wynda waited with her sister, serving as her chaperone.

He wondered if Aila had found a gentleman that would suit among those she danced with. He both wished Aila would for his own peace of mind, and hers, yet he did not care for the notion if she wasn't matched with someone who would treat her well.

"I just wanted to thank you for the loveliest time I have ever had," Aila said. "Thank you." Then she curtseyed and the two of them left.

He wanted to walk them up to their chamber, but then he saw Gustafson greet the women and escort them back inside the keep. Alban hoped the king's steward wouldn't lecture the women.

"I suppose we couldn't just steal her away from

here," Ward said, joining Alban.

He appreciated his brother's comment, but was surprised he sounded half-serious. "The king would want my head and Ronan's too. So nay. Otherwise, I would strongly consider the possibility."

His brother laughed at him, and then they continued to dance until it was very late and they retired for the night.

"We have the hunt to go on with the king on the morrow to replenish the meat for the meals," Alban said.

"Early. He always goes before the sun rises."

"All right. Sounds good to me."

They retired to bed after that. Shortly after both brothers fell asleep, Alban heard a light knocking at their chamber door and wondered what the trouble was now.

CHAPTER 3

"What are we to do?" Aila asked her sister. "The maids are so sick, I think we need to have the king's healer look at them. He has his own physician, but he would probably not agree to him taking care of the maids."

"Aye. But we canna traipse around the castle seeking help either." Wynda wiped cool water over Mai's forehead, the sicker of the two women.

"What if I asked Alban if he would mind enquiring about the healer? His chamber is only two doors down from ours. I could quickly ask him and then return here while he located one."

"All right. But hastily. It would no' look good if you were caught at his chamber door in the middle of the night either."

"Aye." Aila hurried to throw her wool brat over her chemise, and then left the chamber. A sconce lit the corridor, the flames casting shadows about, making it appear as though ghostly figures were floating about her in the hallway.

She quickly made her way to Alban's door, hoping she'd wake him and not his brother. When she knocked, she waited for quite a bit before someone approached the door. She realized her hair was down, not something she had thought of because she was so concerned about their servants.

When Alban pulled the door open, he was bare-chested, wearing his brat belted at the waist, without shoes or a tunic. For a moment, she stared at his beautiful, muscled chest, her heart pounding with worry about being caught alone with a half-naked Highlander, and with concern for her servants.

"Lady Aila." He startled her from her thoughts, then he moved out of his room and closed the door to his chamber. "What is wrong?"

"Oh, aye, our servants are ill. We thought they would be better and looked to be improving earlier today. But tonight they are both feverish, and we canna bring the fever down. I wished to find the healer, but—"

"You canna run around the castle alone. I will go and find one for you. Return—" Alban's words were abruptly cut short when they heard someone's heavy footfalls as he approached.

Feeling panicked, she was afraid she wouldn't make it down the corridor to her room in time before she was caught.

Alban must have assumed the same thing and suddenly moved her against the wall with his hot body pressing indecently close and held her hostage. "Forgive me," he breathed against her cheek. And then he moved his warm lips against her mouth and kissed her.

A lady with the right upbringing would never, ever kiss a gentleman—or an untitled Highlander—let alone do so in the king's own castle when he planned to marry her off to one of his loyal lords. She would never have kissed Alban back—or so she told herself—except to pretend she was not who she was, rather just a servant girl having a good time with one of the king's honored guests.

Yet, she gave into the kiss as if she'd been trained in the art of kissing, which, with the way Alban was kissing her back, she found it easy to follow his lead. She soaked up the feel of his warm mouth against hers, and the smoldering flame that ignited low in her belly and fanned the heat all the way through her, despite the chill in the corridor. His chest pressed against her breasts, making them tingle with the most delicious need. His manhood stirred against her waist, and she realized why her mother had warned her and her sister never to kiss a gentleman in such a manner. Indeed, not until she was wed to him, for she felt urges she'd never known she could experience. Womanly urges that compelled her to take this further.

She wrapped her arms around his neck, Alban's mouth smiling slightly against her lips, as she pressed him tighter. She thought if he was as close as he could be, whoever was about to pass them by—hopefully without stopping to speak—would not see her, as tall as Alban was. Though she was hoping the Highlander would not presume she was always this forward with a man whether she knew him or not. Yet she was thrilled beyond measure to enjoy his attentions, even if it was just to keep her reputation intact. But if the man stopped to speak with Alban, and the Highlander quit kissing her to speak with the person in kind, her character would be in tatters.

"Ahem," the male said, but continued to walk on by.

She didn't dare glance in his direction to see if she knew the man. Alban didn't either, but she wasn't sure if it was because he was so wrapped up in kissing her, or because he was afraid to reveal who she was.

If Alban hadn't been holding her so close, she would have melted right into the stone floor, her body boneless. His breathing was as labored as hers, his heartbeat pounding just as fast. He didn't make a move to release her, waiting while the footfalls faded away. He smelled of summer and the woods, of freshly-washed, earthy male. And then the footsteps were gone.

Yet even then, Alban didn't let her go. "Wait, just a moment more."

She should have wanted to scurry back to her chamber, hide away from the threat of exposure, but she craved being with Alban longer, to enjoy more of this with him.

She did as he told her, kept her arms around his neck, and held him tight as if her life depended on it. Again, she wished the king could consider Alban as a prospect for marriage. If nothing more than she thought he would be a wonderful lover, kind, and protective.

"Okay, we can go now."

But he didn't let her go to her chamber by herself. He rushed her down the corridor, his hand holding hers, warmly, possessively. And she wondered if he'd thought to kiss her closer to her chamber if someone else should suddenly wander through there. She opened the door, and squeezed his hand, her voice breathy when she spoke. "I am in your debt."

He only smiled, his voice husky. "As I am in yours."

The rogue!

Then she moved inside and closed the door, and listened as he moved away from it in a hurry. She leaned against the door, not believing how she'd kissed him, or the trouble they both could have been in if they had been caught.

"Has he gone to fetch the healer?" Wynda asked.

"Aye."

"Tell me you were no' caught with him in the corridor."

"Nay, no' that anyone would know."

"Why are your cheeks so flushed?" Wynda asked, alarmed.

"Someone came. Alban had to..." Aila paused. It was one thing to tell her sister what had happened. Quite another to mention it in front of their servants.

Wynda joined her and whispered, "Had to *what*?"

"Kiss me. We had to kiss, to make it look like Alban was with a servant. That *I* was that servant."

"Och, nay."

"Aye. I am no' ruined. He will say naught of this to anyone. And he has gone to do our bidding."

"I should have been the one to ask for his help."

"Nay."

Wynda's brows shot up. "Because he might have kissed me instead of *you*? The king willna wish you wed to the Highlander, Aila. Remember that."

"Aye, it was only a means to protect me from prying eyes. He was bare-chested, after all."

Aila didn't think she'd ever seen her sister's eyes grow as big as they were right now.

"Of course, you didna kiss him back."

"Oh, aye, of course I did." Aila lifted her chin and folded her arms. "How else was I to pretend to be a serving girl caught up in the rapture of the moment?"

Wynda groaned, and the two of them grabbed wet cloths and each returned to one of their servants to try and cool down their feverish skin.

***

Alban rushed into his chamber and woke Ward. "I must find the king's healer. Lady Aila's servants are sick with fever. I wanted to let you know where I was if you woke and found I was gone." Alban threw on a tunic and refastened his plaid around it.

"I will come with you and we can split forces to locate one." Ward was already out of the bed and dressing.

Soon, they headed out of the chamber and, after descending the stairs, they saw a dark-haired guard approach, his look stern, his hand on the hilt of his sword. They weren't used to guards being about at this time of night, but Alban supposed that since the king was here, it would be prudent.

"Lady Wynda and her sister are in need of a healer. Rather, their maids are," Alban told the guard.

"I will take you to her. Quickly, though."

They passed through to a large chamber where servants were sleeping on pallets and the guard woke one. "Inghean, your services are needed."

Alban explained the situation while she woke a younger woman, who looked at her with bleary eyes.

"Come. This is what being a healer is all about." Then Inghean wrapped her plaid about her and the other woman did likewise.

"She is in-training," Inghean grumbled, sounding as though the training was not going well. Then she grabbed a bag and woke another servant. "Two women are ill. I need you to help me."

While they went about their preparations in the kitchen, the guard returned to his post and Alban and Ward headed back to their chamber. Though Alban continued on to Lady Aila's chamber to let them know the healer, her assistant, and another servant were on their way to aid them.

"Thank you," Aila said, a wet cloth in her hand, her expression hopeful. She was beautiful with her red hair curling over her shoulders as if she'd had a good tumble in bed. "We are forever beholden to you."

"I pray the maids shall recover soon. Did you need anything else of me?"

"Nay. We thank you again."

"Good night, my lady." He bowed deeply to show his utmost respect to her, to let her know that though he had loved kissing her, feeling the passion ignite between them, in no way did he respect her any less for what had happened.

"Good night, Alban."

He took his leave and knew when he retired for the night, all he would think about was the intimacy they had shared and how much he wished for more.

On the way to his chamber, he nodded to the healer and the others who were hurrying to Aila's chamber and then he shut the door to his own. As soon as he returned to his bed, Ward asked, keeping his voice low so only Alban would hear him in the event anyone was listening in, "Just what *did* happen between you and the lady?"

"You were asleep." At least Alban was convinced Ward had been, unless he had pretended to be so he didn't have to answer the door.

"I woke when you left the bed. You were only half dressed when you were standing in the doorway speaking to Lady Aila. And then you went into the corridor with her and shut the door. You were out there with her for what seemed like an interminable time. *Alone.* At least I didna think Lady Wynda was there also."

"She was seeing to the sick servants."

"Then Lady Aila *was* alone with you."

Long silence. Alban knew his brother was pondering the consequences, not that he'd fallen asleep.

"You were lucky no' to have been seen then alone with the lass. You know as many people as there are here for the gathering, there will always be someone who is out and about."

Alban wondered who had seen him with Aila, though at least he believed the man had not known who she was or something would have been said already. Unless it had been a servant and he told someone of importance later.

"You were no' seen, correct?"

Alban had no intention of lying to his brother, though he hadn't intended to talk to him about this if he hadn't asked him directly. "I kissed her so that whoever the man was who passed us by wouldna see her face. Mine, either. Though because we were standing so close to our chamber door, he might have presumed it was me. Or you even."

Ward said not a word.

Alban figured he was thinking on the matter, wondering how to deal with the consequences if something was said on the morrow.

"You are sure the man didna know who she was?"

"I dinna think so."

Ward turned in his bed. "Was she upset with you for taking license?"

"Nay. Grateful. I protected her from prying eyes. But more than that, I was going to find help for their sick maids."

Again there was a prolonged period of silence. Alban was tired and wanted to sleep, but all he could think of was Aila and the way she had so passionately held him tight to her breast and kissed him back.

"Let us hope then that we shall no' find ourselves in chains in the dungeon on the morrow. Good night, brother."

Alban closed his eyes. "You would have done the same."

Ward chuckled. "I imagine I would have, though if it had been me, the lass might have objected quite strenuously."

Alban smiled. At least he hoped the lass would not have wished to kiss his brother.

***

Before Alban was ready to wake that morn, Ward was already rousting him from the bed. "Time for the hunt. We canna be late."

"Aye." Alban loved the hunt, but hunting with the king was a different matter. He hoped he did not breach protocol if he should spy a boar and take off after it when he should leave it to the king. He had not slept well at all last night, not while recalling how Aila had wrapped her arms around his neck and played the role of a smitten serving girl perfectly. Except he didn't think she was just pretending to enjoy the intimacy between them.

He hurried to dress. "I want to stop by the ladies' chamber to see how the maids are faring."

"Aye, but I am going with you to keep you out of trouble in case you have the urge to kiss Lady Aila again."

"What happened last night was out of necessity. It willna happen again."

"Aye," Ward said. "Unless it becomes necessary again."

They left the chamber, headed for the ladies' door, and Alban knocked.

The healer answered the door and Alban was disappointed he was unable to see Aila. But she might have been asleep still, or getting dressed, which was just as well.

"The ladies are sleeping. Their maids are also. They are doing much better this morn. The fever has broken."

"We are glad to hear it," Alban said. "We are off to the hunt, but we will check back with you when we return."

"As you wish," she said, then shut the door.

"To the hunt then, brother. May neither of us do what we ought no' and pay for the mistake." Ward slapped Alban on the back and again Alban would have wished his presence at the king's gathering had not been required, if it had not been for his meeting Lady Aila.

CHAPTER 4

Following the knocking on the chamber door, Aila had heard Alban's voice inquiring as to their maids' condition. She at once wished she'd been dressed and had received the news. Even though it was best that she had not. Not after what had happened between Alban and Aila last night.

Even so, she was glad to hear the maids were well, and she poked at Wynda to wake her. "We are going to be late."

Wynda groaned. "But the maids—"

"The king willna excuse you from the hunt when he intends to arrange marriageable prospects for you. You best be on your way," Inghean said. "We will take care of them while you are gone. You wouldna be able to do anything more for them than we can."

Aila was already dressing, grateful that the maids were getting better, but worried she and her sister might turn up late for the hunt. Despite knowing it was not prudent to show any more interest in Alban, she was hoping to see him anyway.

When she and her sister joined the gathering in the bailey, it was so crowded that she couldn't see Alban for all the other men ready to hunt with the king.

Wynda smiled at her as if knowing just who she was looking for, though she'd warned her again that showing any interest in Alban was a lost cause.

And then she saw him, sitting proud upon his horse, his quiver and bow, sword and dagger ready for a fight, or a hunt. But what thrilled her to no end was that he was watching her and as soon as he caught her eye, he bowed his head a little to her. She gave him a quick smile, and felt her cheeks flush, though she was certain he couldn't tell from the distance he was from her.

Gustafson and several other men glanced in her direction, and Aila turned away for both their sakes, hoping no one would know who Alban had just acknowledged with a courtly greeting.

And then they moved off to the woods to hunt.

A lady riding near her commented, "'Tis a shame Alban would never be considered acceptable for a lady to marry."

Aila glanced at her, wondering just how she had come to that conclusion. Lady Felicia was also eligible for marriage, dark-haired, her dark eyes and lips smiling in an amused way. Then Aila recalled the dancing and how she had danced with Alban so many times. She almost breathed a sigh of relief that the woman's comment had nothing to do with the incident outside Alban's chamber.

"A rumor is circulating that he is quite the lady's man," Lady Felicia said.

Aila tried not to allow the woman's words to upset her. Aila should have realized he might be, as handsome and charming as he was. Not to mention the way he kissed her so exquisitely had to mean he was well-versed in the activity.

"They say he was with a woman in the corridor last eve."

Aila's heart practically quit beating.

"You have a chamber with your sister down that same corridor, do you no'?" Felicia raised a brow. "I heard you had some trouble with your servants and Alban came to their rescue."

Word sure spread around the king's court quickly. "He did. And the maids are recovering thanks to him, the healer, her assistant, and the other woman who helped them."

"Then he must have been interrupted with his business with the maid. The king's steward didna know who she was, but as happens in a court, with all the intrigue that goes on here, he is attempting to learn the truth of the matter. He asked Alban, of course. But the rogue said he hadna even learned her name. Some women are so wanton."

Aila's face burned with mortification. Was the woman fishing for the truth? Watching her reaction?

Wondering if she were the woman, or if it would upset Aila that he was such a "rogue" with regard to seeing other women? Despite the seriousness of the situation, she couldn't help but be glad the woman he had been with was none other than her, and not some other.

"You are interested in Lord Dunlap, are you no'?" Aila asked, changing the subject. She wondered if Aila's dancing with the lord had irked Felicia. She hoped it had.

Felicia shrugged. "I am interested in many, as many are interested in me. They say 'tis because of my beautiful dark tresses for one. Though I have many other qualities they are interested in."

"Indeed." Aila couldn't imagine even one. The woman had to have everyone do everything for her as if she was incapable of doing anything for herself. She couldn't imagine what she would have done if her maids had become ill on the journey here.

"I am glad no' to have fiery red hair. It must cause you much grief."

Not if the way Alban seemed to like her just as she was, if that was any indication.

Wynda was on the other side of Aila, listening to the conversation. She cast Aila a small smile.

The sky was beginning to lighten as everyone grew quiet, moving through the woods to search for prey. None of the women were hunting, just being there to show they supported the men in the hunt. Not that Aila and her sister couldn't, but the king didn't wish it. Even the men had to be careful they didn't take down the king's own prey.

She noted that all the men were concentrating on hunting, any interest in the women all but forgotten.

They rode along until they spied boars in the woods and the men took chase. The ladies followed them, not wanting to fall behind, though a couple of men were watching over them, serving as guards. When three of the other women did lose sight of the hunters, the guards dropped back to ensure they remained protected.

Aila was glad that one of the women who could not keep up was none other than Felicia.

Servants began taking care of the boar struck down to return it to the castle, while the king and the rest of the men continued to hunt. As many people had come for the gathering, the men would need to hunt several more for the feast.

Wynda veered off to get closer to one of the lords she'd danced with and Aila wondered if she was interested in marrying the man. He looked to be much younger than her deceased husband and just as braw as Alban. Then movement near a pond, half hidden behind brambles, caught Aila's eye.

She paused and stared at the creature. A rare white red hart. A mythical white stag that made her heart sing with joy. But what if the hunters or the king learned of it? They would kill it, believing it would give them special powers, most likely. Though she knew she should not do so, she had to take the chance to save it—at least from the hunt this time--and slipped away from the others, meaning to scare the stag off before anyone was aware of its existence.

Yet, for a moment as she grew close, he only watched her. She couldn't believe he did not run away. She just gloried in the presence of him. Then she heard someone coming, and she rode close to the hart, hating to scare it off, but she had to so that she could protect it.

He dashed off, and she turned to see who had followed her, worried it was one of the guards who would tell on her—that he'd witnessed her scaring off the rarest of beasts. He'd probably say it all had to do with the curse of her red hair.

Yet when she saw him riding toward her, she was both relieved and worried to see Alban joining her. Before she could return the way she had come, he leapt down from his horse, helped her down from hers, then tied her reins and his to a branch, and quickly whispered, "Someone is coming."

"But wouldna it be better to—"

"Be seen riding alone together?"

"Aye, than to be seen dismounted and whispering sweet secrets to each other," she said, frowning at him.

He smiled, but then grew serious again. He motioned due north of them, then moved in close to her. "A couple of men went this way. I didna want to risk us trying to rejoin the others just yet. If we go back, the guards walking with the ladies who could not keep up with the hunt could run into us."

His whispered breath tickled her ear and she had the worst urge to wrap her arms around his neck and kiss him again. Though this time, she would not be able to pretend she was a servant if anyone caught them.

They moved deeper into the brush and waited. "You know the king wouldna be pleased that you chased away a prized white hart."

She frowned at him. Did he intend to tell on her?

"I would have done the same thing," he continued in a hushed voice.

She let out her breath. "He was beautiful, was he no'?"

"Aye, a miracle to observe and I was glad to see you shoo him away, after I had a chance to see him too."

He held her close as they grew quiet again. But when they heard men's voices nearby, her heart filled with dread. Surely, they would be caught and she would be ruined. She suspected the king wouldna like it, but he would probably still force her to marry someone not of her choice. Maybe someone who would really despise her for her transgressions, as innocent as they were.

"We canna try to kill him again," one of the men gruffly said. "It would appear suspect if we tried too soon."

"Then some other way. Aye. Come, we must join the others."

The men rode off, but Aila and Alban stayed where they were, waiting.

"Are they talking about the hunt?" She didn't think

so, but she wanted Alban to confirm what she was worried about. They intended to kill someone. But who?

"I doubt it. But we canna let them know we overheard them either."

"Do you know who they are?"

"Nay. I didna recognize the voices. Their words were spoken too low." Alban helped her onto her horse.

"Should we leave here separately?"

"Nay. I wouldna leave you to travel by yourself. You could be in danger, should you run upon the two conspirators, and they believed you had overheard them. At least I am armed and can take care of them."

"Even if they are lords?"

"Aye, even so."

"We should learn who they are."

"For now, I only wish to return you to the hunt without raising any speculation about us being alone together."

"I am sorry, Alban. I didna mean to put you in this position."

"I am no'. Being with you has made the gathering worthwhile. Though I didna want to come and I was eager to leave, I will miss seeing your cheerful smiles."

"'Tis too bad I am no' just a serving girl," she said, although it didn't mean he would be interested in marrying her if she had been.

"If you were, I would steal you away."

She smiled then, loving his comment. But then as they moved through the forest, hearing shouts ahead, they both grew quiet again.

They saw the guards with the ladies who were riding slower, and nudged their horses in another direction. They had gone far enough away from the others so that they could not be seen when she spied a wild boar and motioned to it.

He nodded, and called for men to join in the hunt. "Go north. I saw some women and men up that way and just fall in behind them. I will chase after the boar and give everyone the location. Everyone will be running every which way so no one will notice you were not with a group of ladies. Go."

He took off in the direction of the boar, shouting where it was, but Aila figured it was better to pretend she had heard him shouting and joined in on the hunt. Well, racing after the boar, not truly hunting it. She would not be left behind.

Several others joined her, including a couple of the men whom she'd danced with, who were now smiling a little to see her doing so well at keeping up. But then her sister joined her and didn't look like she was really happy with her.

Had she seen Aila with Alban? Or was Wynda just upset with her for not staying by her side and for disappearing for a time? Probably. Wynda had always thought it was her duty to look out for her younger sister.

All that mattered was that no one suspected she'd been with Alban alone, and that the men who'd been talking about killing someone didn't learn she and Alban had overheard them, especially if they were referring to a man and not about something they were hunting.

She considered confiding in Wynda, but she assumed the fewer who knew the better. She surely didn't want to put her own sister in harm's way.

Still, every time Aila heard a man's voice, she wondered—was he one of the men who had spoken? And intended to kill someone?

***

As soon as possible, Alban needed to tell his brother what he and Aila had overheard. He needed to speak to her about it too, to tell her to pretend she'd heard nothing. He and his brother would look into it as quietly as they could. But he didn't want her involved in it in any way.

Though he was certain his brother would not be pleased that Alban had been alone with the lass again. But when Alban had caught sight of her slipping away on her own, he'd had every intention of bringing her back to where the rest of the hunting party had been. His first thought had been that she'd spied something interesting and she'd slipped off to see it. He never would have believed he'd see the wondrous white stag. Maybe a butterfly, or something like that, had caught her eye. He understood her need to save the hart. To send it on its way. But still, she risked her own life by doing so if the men had realized she was nearby.

He could just imagine how angry the king would

have been too, if he had learned she had chased away the stag when he could have hunted it as the find of his lifetime.

"The find is yours," Gustafson shouted to Alban, still in the lead as he chased the boar down. "The king is otherwise occupied."

"Lady Aila's find rather," Alban shouted back, though he heard another rider approaching as if to take the lead.

"Indeed," the king's steward said, sounding surprised.

Lord Dunlap charged past Alban, knocking into him as if to unseat Alban, but he was prepared for the assault and managed to balance his weight to keep from flying from the saddle.

Alban had hunted boar before. He knew how unpredictable they could be, which was why he'd kept a respectable distance from the raging beast. Sure enough, the boar turned and charged Dunlap's mount. In panic, Dunlap's horse reared up. The lord lost his balance and fell to the ground, as Alban distracted the boar to save the man's life, moving in between the boar and Dunlap, still lying on the ground. Had he injured himself?

Alban shot the boar twice, slowing him until others arrived to help finish the job. Making the honorable gesture, Alban dismounted and went to Dunlap's aid, but he slapped Alban's hand away and unsteadily got to his feet. Ward had retrieved Dunlap's spooked horse and handed the reins to him. Two of Dunlap's friends arrived to help him remount his horse. From the way the earl was limping, it seemed he'd sprained an ankle in the fall.

With a smirk, all Alban could think of was that the lord would no longer be able to dance with Lady Aila during his stay here, then he climbed into his saddle and saw the lady and her sister watching him. Had she told Lady Wynda about what they'd overheard in the woods? He hoped not. She looked concerned and he hoped to alleviate her worry over this matter as soon as he could. But he would do so when his brother was present.

After the king declared they had caught enough boar, they headed back to the keep. Some of their fellow hunters had been injured in the hunt. At least five men had been gored. A couple more had injuries like Lord Dunlap's. Sim, one of the king's servants, had been the unlucky target of some hunter's arrow, though the shot had only hit him in the arm, not as bad as it could have been. No one had claimed the arrow, undoubtedly not wanting to admit to making the mistake. Some lords blamed the servant for getting in the way. Alban couldn't abide by some men's attitudes when it came to servants.

Yet he knew it was possible they could examine the arrow and see if anyone had arrows made in the same way as that one. If anyone cared. He frowned. What if the men's secret claim in the woods that they hadn't killed the man and couldn't try again had all to do with the servant? Had the shooter meant to kill Sim because he knew something the lord wished kept secret? If the person speaking had been a lord? Or had the servant gotten in the way of his real target?

He had to learn the truth.

Half the women had already returned to the castle. Only five remained with the hunting party. Among all of the women, Lady Aila was the only one who had found prey for the hunt.

"Shall we go now, brother?" Ward glanced from him to Aila as if he was aware something more was going on between them.

"Aye. As long as we escort the ladies back to the castle." Alban didn't want to let Aila out of his sight.

***

Aila was glad Alban and his brother were accompanying them back to the keep. It wasn't like they were alone by any means, as everyone headed back in. But she felt safer knowing the brothers would protect them if anything bad should happen.

The weather had been beautiful for the hunt, but the once fluffy clouds drifting through the sky had begun to take over the whole of the sky and were darkening by the minute. The hunting party would be drenched soon, she was sure. There was no hope for reaching the shelter of the castle in time, but at least they had finished the hunt, so they could return and dry off.

"You made a great find, Lady Aila," Ward said, and she was afraid her face blanched as worried as she was that Alban had told his brother they had discovered the white stag. He frowned at her when she seemed so concerned about his comment.

Alban quickly said, "The boar."

"Oh, aye."

Now it sounded as if Alban had made it up that she had seen it first.

"I was glad to be of some assistance during the hunt," she easily said, when in reality she had let the most exquisite creature get away.

Ward was still watching her curiously. Her sister was now also. Aila was still trying to decide for sure if she could even tell Wynda about the white stag. What could she say? That only she had seen it? And then her sister would know she'd been alone, and risked her neck to keep the hunters from learning about it. Or tell her that Alban had seen it too, to verify she truly had witnessed the elusive creature. But that would mean she had been alone with him, again. And what else had they done? Witnessed a plot to kill someone, which Aila didn't want to reveal to her sister either.

"You did well to keep up with the hunt," Ward said.

"Our da had always insisted, in the event we were married, and our husbands were away, we would lead the hunting party. At least that was the idea." Aila wished her sister would say something and not leave it up to her to do all the talking.

Maybe Wynda was just tired after the late night they'd had with their servants. Aila was eager to get back to them, to see how they were faring.

"If you dinna believe it is an imposition, we would like to check on you later to learn how your servants are doing," Alban said.

Aila ran her hands over her kirtle, smoothing the fabric, though it was fine. "Aye, it would be kind of you to do so."

And then Lord Gustafson joined them. "It was remarkable how Lady Aila found a boar on her own. I am much impressed not only that you kept up with the men, but also managed to finish with us also. How did you like the hunt?"

"I enjoyed it very much," Aila said and Wynda agreed.

"I understand your maids have been ill though. When we return, the healer and her assistant will have to see to the men wounded on the hunt. I hope that will not cause you any trouble," the king's steward said.

"Nay, they were getting better when we left. The injured men will need caring for at once when they return. We will see to our maids," Wynda said.

"You will be expected at the feast. I will ensure a couple of servants watch over your servants in the meantime."

"Thank you," Wynda said.

"I saw you near Lord Farquharson at one point, Lady Wynda. But I didna see Lady Aila for a time."

"I canna imagine how you could keep an eye on everyone at the same time. My sister rode off to catch up with someone and I didna want to intrude if she wished to speak with a gentleman suitor for a time."

"Ah."

Gustafson's sharp eyes shifted to settle on Alban. "You had the honor of taking down the boar. 'Twas a shame Lord Dunlap was injured in the process."

"Aye." Alban didn't say anything further and Aila suspected he was biting his tongue.

She was still furious with the lord for running into Alban, trying to unseat him. She was glad the dark-haired earl now had mud on his clothes and even in his hair from where he had landed on the wet earth. Did the other lords feel it served Alban right for having the honor to take down the boar when he was not even titled? Probably.

So it served Lord Dunlap right for falling from his own horse. Though she was glad the boar had not gored him. It was only through Alban's quick actions and risking his own life that the lord had been saved from an even worse injury. Death even. Would the man thank him for saving his life? No. She hoped the king would not choose him for her husband.

"Did you see how Alban saved Lord Dunlap?" She hoped that he had witnessed the Highlander's brave actions for himself.

"Aye. I am no' sure I could have reacted as quickly."

She was glad he'd seen it for himself. She wanted to add that Alban had acted honorably the whole time while Lord Dunlap had not, but she knew the king's steward would not care. Lord Dunlap was a man of position and power so he could act that way toward those who were beneath him and no one could say a word against it.

"The king is motioning to me. I must go. We will see you at the meal." Then the king's steward rode off to join Malcolm.

Aila was relieved. She always felt like she was under Gustafson's scrutiny whenever he was around. But with Alban, she felt comfortable. Able to talk to him about practically anything. Just like she was with her sister...usually.

A light shower began and they raced off for the castle, trying to beat the heavier downpour. By the time they reached the portcullis, the heavens had let loose the denser rain.

Aila and her sister were laughing, remembering the good times they'd had in the pouring rain. By the time lads had taken their horses, as well as Alban and his brother's, they were well drenched.

The men escorted them up the stairs, Alban promising again to check on them once they were out of their wet clothes.

As soon as Aila and her sister entered their chamber, they saw their maids sitting up and eating and were delighted.

Before Aila could ask them how they felt, Wynda turned to Aila, her brow deeply furrowing. "What happened to you when I lost you?"

CHAPTER 5

While they changed into dry clothes in their chamber, Alban quietly told his brother what he and Aila had overheard in the woods.

His brother frowned at him. "You are certain no one saw you go off with Lady Aila alone?"

Alban was irritated with his brother. "Ward, that is the least of my concern right now. And nay. No one else saw her slip off. Only I did. We have to learn who has plans to kill whom and stop them."

Ward rubbed his whiskered chin, his brow furrowed. "You dinna recognize either of the voices?"

"They were speaking low and even if they were no', I doubt I would have recognized them. No' unless they were one of our own men. I wondered if the shooting of the servant on the hunt was by accident or by design. Mayhap he was the one they had targeted, but they failed to kill him." Alban finished belting his plaid.

"If that is so, why?"

"He knows something about the men and they need to keep him from talking? Or mayhap he got in their way when they intended to shoot someone else. Did you see the incident?" Alban sat on the bed to pull on his socks and shoes.

"Nay. We had split off after three boars running in different directions. Two of the men who tried to finish the boar we took down were gored. The boar only missed me by the length of a tusk. I truly thought I would be run through if it hadna been for some baron I didna know who shot the boar and finally took him down. Unlike in Lord Dunlap's case with you, I profusely thanked the man." Ward sat down on the chair to put on his socks and shoes.

"Then I am just as thankful you were safe and unharmed during the hunt as well. I didna have a chance to tell Lady Aila that we would look into this. That I want her to have no part in it if she thinks to try to help identify the men," Alban said.

"Aye, I agree. 'Tis entirely possible the man who was shot wasna part of the other men's discussion. That Sim was just accidentally shot." Ward rose from the chair and crossed the floor to the window.

"True. Then who had they attempted to kill and not succeeded?"

"They could have been talking about an earlier incident. No' anything to do with the hunt." Ward peered out the window for a moment, then turned around.

Alban ran his hands through his hair. "You are right. I want to place one of our men as guard on the servant who was shot, just in case he truly is the target." He felt they had to protect the man in case he was the one targeted for some reason.

"You will arouse unnecessary suspicion if you do. Mayhap we can ask if the servant can serve us for a time while he is recovering from his wound. He willna be much use on the king's staff. One of our men can safeguard him here, in our chamber, until we learn the truth of the matter. If the servant wasna the one who was targeted, who was?"

"Any of the lords, the king even, could have grievances against them. We need to learn who witnessed the shooting of the servant." Alban would not let go of the notion until they knew for sure what was going on.

Ward let out his breath. "Aye, but again, inquiries could cause speculation."

"We have to do something."

"If we are to get at the root of this, we have to be cautious though, or show our hand."

Alban didn't want to be cautious. He wanted to expose the assassins for what they were before anyone else could get hurt.

"When I mentioned that it was great that Lady Aila had located the boar, you had to remind her of it. What was that all about?" Ward asked.

Alban loved the way she had been concerned for the stag's safety, though he didn't like that she'd gone off by herself alone. "She had located a white stag first."

"Nay." Ward looked incredulous.

"Aye. We couldna allow anyone to learn about it. Certainly, that we saw it and didna let the king know."

"Truly? A white stag? I should have loved to have seen it."

"He was truly remarkable. Let us see to the women then, and afterward, inquire about the servant." Alban was eager to learn what they could as soon as they could.

When they reached Aila's chamber, Alban was glad to see the two ladies' maids, Mai and Ralene, sitting up and eating at a table, smiling and talking.

"They are doing well." Aila led the brothers back into the corridor. After she shut the door, she spoke low to them. "What are we to do about...you know what?"

Alban explained what they intended to do about the wounded servant. Aila looked so relieved and he was glad she was pleased and that he had suggested it.

"I worry about Sim," she said.

"You didna check on him, did you?" Alban's heart began to pound with worry for her safety.

"Nay. Wynda wouldna let me."

The lass was far too willing to risk her life, and he had to impress upon her that he and his brother would take care of the matter. "You wouldna have gone alone, would you, my lady?"

"Nay. Of course no'. I would have taken my sister."

He let out his breath. "My lady…"

"Aye, I didna go anywhere, but I still did worry about him. May I go with you now?"

"We are trying no' to arouse suspicions," Ward warned her. "If all of us were to go at the same time, it would look too irregular."

"Aye." She wrung her hands. "Mayhap I can make inquiries about Sim's injury. I could act"—she shuddered—"morbidly interested."

"My lady," Alban said, wanting to sequester her away to keep her out of harm's way. "Is it no' enough that *we* look into this matter?"

Full of worry, her soft brown eyes watched him, and then she nodded. "Aye, of course. 'Tis your place no' mine to look into such a despicable plan, if it were an attempt at assassination. Do keep me informed, will you no'?"

"Definitely. We must hurry to see about Sim now. And mayhap we can speak later." If they could do so without garnering undo attention.

Then Alban and Ward took their leave, but Alban worried the lady was not satisfied with their plan.

When she returned to her chamber and shut the door, Ward asked, "Did you get the impression the lady has a mind of her own?"

"Aye." Which Alban loved in a woman as long as it didn't mean endangering her life.

***

Aila would not be dissuaded from inquiring about the incident when the servant was shot. She first asked the ladies who had attended the hunt and had kept up. She was convinced none of the ladies would be involved in anything so diabolical. And she was certain none of them would share what Aila was questioning them about. They were at the meal now, and she managed to learn that Lady Umberton had witnessed the entire event. Eagerly, Aila asked her to sit with her and Wynda to tell them all about it. The lady was all too happy to oblige. Hopefully she wouldn't embellish the story too much.

Wynda nudged Aila's ankle under the table, but she ignored her. This was the first lead she'd had, and she'd spoken already to Alban, his brother, and her sister as well, about the servant's recollection. But he had seen nothing but the boar coming at him and then realized an arrow had lodged in his arm. Beyond that, all he had tried to do was stay out of the path of the boar.

"Do tell me what you saw exactly," Aila said enthusiastically.

"Well," the lady said, her blue eyes widening with eagerness as she appeared delighted to tell Aila and her sister something they wished to know, "'twas just an accident, of course."

"Aye, of course. The servant must have gotten in the way of the lord." Aila didn't know if the shooter was a lord or someone like Alban. But she thought if she pretended to know he was a lord, the woman would clarify who, or maybe say he was not, and tell her his name to set her straight.

"Oh, for sure."

"I am positive he must have told the man he was sorry." Aila knew he had not come forth about the matter at all.

"You jest. If anything, he might be grousing about missing his target, disparaging the servant's name."

"Is he?"

"How would I know that for certain? He would probably tell his close circle of male friends. Certainly not a topic of conversation for the women."

Was that a rebuke because Aila was asking about it? "Who else was on the ground when the boar was charging?"

"Why the king, of course. Which is why I am confident whoever shot the servant would have been angry with him as he tried to shoot the boar to protect the king."

Aila closed her gaping mouth. Had the hunter tried to shoot the king himself? She had to get word to Alban and his brother soonest. She glanced in Alban's direction where he was seated with his brother again and realized he had been studying her. She wondered if he suspected she was trying to learn what had gone on during the incident. She wasn't going to leave it to the men to find out if she had a chance to safely discover anything.

"How come the king was on foot? Had he fallen?" Aila asked. It was an honest question. Lord Dunlap had fallen from his horse when the horse had reared up at the sight of the raging boar.

"Heavens no. And dinna say that to anyone. The king had gallantly dismounted to give the killing blow to the boar, but it had other plans." Lady Umberton drank from her tankard of sweet, honeyed mead.

Aila wanted desperately to ask if Lady Umberton knew which direction the arrow had flown, and if it could have been meant for the king. But she could not ask her that or the word would surely spread throughout the court that Aila thought the king's life had been in danger.

Lady Umberton probably wouldn't have known anyway, as much of a threat as the boar had been to everyone in the area at the time. They talked about the festivities after that and the dance. Lady Umberton even confided in them about how Lady Felicia was secretly hoping for Lord Dunlap's proposition to the king, asking for her hand in marriage.

"Will he offer for her?" Aila asked, curious. She wasn't truly interested in any of the lords here. Only, with one beautiful Highlander who made her heart beat with passion, and took such a genuine interest in her, their servants, and now the injured servant, she couldn't think of anything else.

"He wasna impressed with her inability to keep up with the hunt. He wants more than a pretty lass who will smile sweetly and agree with everything he says and does. I have heard he has shown some interest in you even. He was much impressed that you no' only kept up with the hunt, but that you found a boar. Lady Felicia isna happy with that at all. Dinna be surprised if she attempts to sabotage your chances at marrying the earl."

Though Aila wasn't interested in the earl, she had no desire to be made the fool of, if Felicia intended to do something to ridicule her.

"I have heard we are going to have races across the loch one of these days when the weather is grand like it was earlier today on the hunt." Lady Umberton ate some of her boar.

"I look forward to it." Aila loved the water. Both she and her sister did. When they were younger, they swam all the time, with guards, naturally, and their maids and mother present. She and Wynda had also learned how to use oars so they could row a boat. They had even raced their da and some of their clansmen in fun. Though they had not been strong enough to beat any of the men, they had all had a good time trying to. Their mother felt it important that a lady know how to do many things well, that mayhap another family would feel was not ladylike at all.

"Do you know this Alban of the Clan Daziel?" Lady Umberton asked. "He seems to have caught your eye. We wondered if he was a childhood friend."

Aila wasn't surprised others had been gossiping about her. She wished she could say they were. To explain some of the familiarity between them. But she couldn't make up stories for she knew she would get caught up in the lie.

"He most graciously offered to assist us in bringing the healer to our chamber so that she could take care of our sick maids," Wynda said.

Lady Umberton smiled sweetly, but her smile didn't appear to be genuine. "Then you danced with him in gratitude."

Aila was certain the lady knew that was not so and was trying to catch her up in a lie. "On the contrary. He asked me to dance before that. He so gallantly wanted to dance with me when no one else would. He is a true gentleman."

"I see. Well, I do suppose his interest in you is only because he canna marry you. Or mayhap he has the ridiculous notion the king will allow him, a commoner, to marry you and take all your properties. Though, I highly doubt it. No' unless Alban has resources and fighting men to call his own to help support the king's cause."

Which Aila was sure he didn't have. He was just a good man. Unfortunately, that would not be good enough for the king.

When the dinner was done, Wynda glowered at Aila. "What?" Aila mouthed, exasperated.

They were alone in the great hall, as much as anyone could be in a castle filled with people, though most everyone had already left. Just Ward and Alban were headed their way.

"You are acting too interested in what happened to the servant. If someone did try to—" Wynda paused as Alban and Ward joined them. "Should you be seen speaking with us here?" She sounded cross.

"My sister worries needlessly when we do have news that you must hear." Aila explained about the king having dismounted when the servant was shot.

"I thought—" Alban said, sounding exasperated with her.

"I said naught that would cause us trouble."

"She didna mention you at all. Just was curious about the man who had shot the servant. But she is liable to get us both in trouble if she keeps this up," Wynda said.

"I hadna planned to ask anyone else. Just the women. And only the one had witnessed the scene."

"Lady Aila—" Alban said.

"I must see to our maids." With that, Aila made her way past the men, her sister hurrying to catch up to her.

"They are right. I am right."

"And how would we know what we now know if I hadna asked her some questions about this?" Aila asked her sister.

"We know naught more than before," Wynda said, sounding annoyed.

"Except that we now know who had dismounted and may have been the target!" Why couldn't everyone see how important that could be?

But Aila didn't intend to go straight back to their chamber. She knocked on the door to Alban and Ward's chamber. "'Tis me, Lady Aila." She glanced at her sister standing next to her, her arms folded across her chest.

"And Lady Wynda. We wish to speak to the wounded man again."

"Aye, my lady," Alban's guard said, opening the door.

The ladies hurried inside and he shut the door. Sim was lying on a pallet, awake, his arm bandaged, his blue eyes wide. "I have never been treated so well after being injured."

"Did you try to save the king while the boar chased you?" Aila asked.

"The king was near me, but you must understand in a situation like that, 'tis every man for himself. We both were trying to avoid the boar's lethal tusks."

"Do you have any enemies?"

The man's mouth gaped. "What makes you ask that?"

"Just in case you had gotten on the bad side of some lord and he shot you instead of the boar," Aila explained. She swore Wynda groaned softly beside her, and the guard looked askance at Aila.

"No' that I recall, my lady. I try always to try to be careful of what I say or do around the noblemen and the ladies. Or I would pay for it for certain."

A knock on the door had everyone turning to look at it. The guard said, "Aye?"

"'Tis me and Ward," Alban said.

Aila figured Alban wouldn't like it that she had questioned the servant any longer. But with her suspicions of the king being in danger, she had to learn if the man recalled anything further about it. Or if he might have had enemies and the attack had nothing to do with the king.

"Thank you," she said to Sim, and headed for the door.

When the guard opened it, Alban was ready to walk in with his brother, but stopped short at seeing her standing there with her sister. "Good day to you, sir," she said, and waited for him to move out of her path.

He bowed and stepped aside. When his brother entered the chamber, Alban shut the door and escorted the women back to their chamber, asking what she had spoken to the servant about. As soon as she told him, he groaned even louder than Wynda had.

"My sentiments exactly," her sister said.

"Lady Aila, I will keep you informed about everything I am doing concerning the matter."

"That is all I can ask for." But Aila had every intention of listening to the men to try and determine who might have shot Sim. And whom the hunter seemed to have a close association with.

CHAPTER 6

Alban had to secure the arrow that had shot Sim, just in case the shooting wasn't an accident. Ward was going to go with him, but Alban thought they'd be less conspicuous if only one of them looked for the arrow.

"If you find it, how will you conceal it?"

"Under my plaid. 'Tis the only way. Unless I wrap it in a bit of cloth, but even that might seem suspicious."

"You canna carry a quiver of arrows, or that would also look odd."

"I agree. Though the healer might have broken it to remove it." Alban grabbed a piece of cloth and tucked it under his plaid, just in case. Then his brother wished him luck and Alban left.

When Alban arrived at the outer building set aside for the wounded men from the hunt, he greeted the healer and asked, "Perchance, do you still have the arrow that struck Sim?"

"The bloody cloths are over there." Inghean waved in the direction of a bucket. "But those will be washed and reused. Mayhap it was tossed…" She rested her chin in her hand as if trying to decide where she might have thrown it. "I removed the arrow from his arm when he was lying over there. Your men came and took him to your chamber to work for you." She raised her brows a tad. "Are you getting much work out of him?"

"He is recovering nicely." Alban wished his men had remembered to ask for the arrow then. They were supposed to, but they had been worried about arousing even more suspicion as to why they were moving him to Alban and his brother's chamber, that they had forgotten to ask about the arrow.

She gave him a little smile. "I am glad to hear it. You might look around on the floor over there. Mayhap I tossed it there. Unless my assistant or some other threw it away."

"Thank you." He tried not to show how interested he was in the arrow.

Inghean looked around at the sleeping, injured men and quietly added, "Someone else was looking for it after I removed it. What need have you of the arrow?"

"A memento for Sim so he can tell wild tales of how he was nearly gored by a boar only to be shot then by a hunter's arrow."

She narrowed her eyes at him. "You were no' there when he was shot. You were…elsewhere."

"Aye." But Alban desperately wanted to know who

had come seeking the arrow. Who else would be interested but the one who had used it on Sim? Trying to cover his tracks lest someone would think he was trying to kill him or someone else, like the king?

"I canna see Sim wanting the arrow for that reason. Might there be another reason?" the healer asked slyly.

"No' one that I can offer."

She pulled him into a little room off the main one and shut the door. "Do you believe someone was trying to kill Sim?"

"Or he got in the way of someone else whom the perpetrator was trying to shoot. Who came for the arrow?"

"A man I dinna know. He was a servant, not a lord. Not one of the king's men. I thought it odd that he would ask for it. And here you are now asking for the very same arrow."

"I must learn who it belongs to."

"Then the arrow pieces are yours. Find who injured Sim. He is a good man, hard-working, and wishes to marry a slip of a woman who is trying diligently to learn how to be a proper healer. I believe you when you say Sim is recovering, and I know you didna ask the king's permission to move him to your chamber to work. What would he do there for you? Especially when he canna use his arm for now. You took him there to question him and to protect him, aye?"

"Aye, but no one must know of this."

"In the event the person who shot him might want

you and your brother dead. I understand completely." Inghean rustled through blankets and various size cloths, until she paused, and wriggled her fingers a little under the bundle of material, then finally extracted half the arrow. "The other half is in here too. I saved it after the other man came looking for it. I told him it had been used for kindling. Seemingly satisfied, he went away. How will you conceal the broken arrow?"

Someone tapped on the door, and Inghean quickly hid them back underneath the cloths. "Aye?"

The door opened and there stood Aila, her eyes growing big to see Alban speaking with Inghean.

"Pray tell me you are no' alone." Alban wanted to take her by the arm and move her straight back to her chamber.

"Nay. Mai was feeling the need to get out and walk a bit and so we came by to thank Inghean for saving her life."

It was possible the lady was telling the truth. But what if she had another motive. That she was seeking the arrow as well?

"What are *you* doing here?" Aila asked.

Alban almost smiled. He hadn't expected *her* to ask *him* to explain his business to her.

Mai quickly thanked Inghean for all her help, and then she quietly left the room so Aila could shut the door. "I am here seeking the arrow. If we dinna get it before whoever..." Aila paused.

"Alban has told me why he wished it too. Mayhap

you can each have half—"

"Nay. The lady doesna need to be involved in this. 'Tis too dangerous."

"Aye, true enough." Inghean retrieved the arrow pieces, but Aila looked them over carefully while Alban pulled out his cloth to hide them.

"Mayhap I should carry them for us, in case anyone stops you for some reason." Aila looked up at him with such sincerity, he couldn't believe the lass was so willing to risk her life for him.

"Lady Aila…"

"Or no'. I was just thinking that it might be easier to conceal them under my long kirtle, than it would for you to hide it beneath your plaid." She suddenly blushed.

He hadn't wanted to think of how the remnants of the arrow would be hidden underneath her kirtle, just as he imagined her own thoughts had drifted that way concerning hiding the arrow parts beneath his garments. He couldn't stop thinking about how she would strap them to her leg. About how he would want to tie it on— to make sure it didn't slip when she walked. What would happen then? She would walk and the arrow halves in the cloth would suddenly appear at her feet?

He didn't like the notion she would carry the evidence that could prove one of the lords had used it on Sim and maybe for a darker purpose than that. Yet her suggestion had merit. He had taken so long to respond, she took the cloth and wrapped the arrow pieces up so that they would be safe to wear. And then she took a couple of long strips of cloth the healer had that would be used to bind wounds. "I will return these when I have accomplished the task," she told Inghean.

Alban folded his arms. "Very well. Be sure to secure it well and I will walk you and your maid back to my chamber—to your chamber, rather—where you can remove it and hand it over to me."

"Mayhap *you* should tie it on to ensure it is perfectly secure," Inghean said.

He knew she had to be jesting, but he swore both women smiled so wickedly, his face flushed with heat. He cleared his throat and removed himself from the room. If she hadn't been a lady, and if he'd already spoken for her—had he been able to—he would have secured it himself, just to be sure it remained where it should.

The women seemed to take forever, and then Aila opened the door. She took a few unsure steps, her hand going to her thigh as if she intended to hold the arrow in place before it dropped to the floor.

He took her hand and led her back into the small room. "Either I wear it, or I secure it to you so that it doesna slip from your person and cause undue concern."

"Do you wish me to chaperone?" Inghean said.

"Aye," Alban said.

"Nay," Aila said. "If you leave the room, you willna see what happens exactly. So if you are questioned, we were all here and we all left after thanking you for being such a great healer."

Inghean shook her head. "Young people these days." Then she left the room and shut the door.

"Do be quick about it," Aila urged and she was blushing furiously.

"Can you lift your kirtle so that my hands will be free to tie on the bundle?"

"Aye," she said, sounding a little unsure of herself.

He rested his hands on her shoulders. "I can carry it, Aila. You need no' worry about it."

"Nay, I still think this is the best plan."

She began to lift her kirtle slowly, and he thought just how sensual she looked as if she were trying to seduce him, when he assumed the way her cheeks turned crimson she was only embarrassed.

"Here, let me." He slid his hands up her thigh to where she'd had the arrow pieces secured, but they were already slipping. Then he removed them. "I will place this around your waist, beneath your kirtle, so that it willna slip below your hips."

She held her kirtle up, her chemise still covering her, and he tied the pouch that they'd created so that it hung down from a makeshift belt against her waist. It shouldn't slip from that position.

As soon as he pulled her kirtle down, he looked to make sure the bundle was not visible. It wasn't.

"You will tell no one of this, will you?"

He smiled at her. "Nay. You are beautiful, my lady. Everything about you is. If I could offer for you, I would in a heartbeat."

She wrapped her arms around his neck, tilted her head back, and waited for a kiss.

At least that's what he assumed she wanted. He certainly wasn't going to ask. Well aware he couldn't take very much longer with her alone in the room, as much as he wanted to, or her maid and the healer would believe he'd made love to the lass as well, he leaned down and kissed her. She kissed him back so passionately, he knew this was what he wanted in his life. A lass like her. Not like her, this one, because he knew he'd never find one again who was just like her.

She parted her lips for his kiss and he slipped inside and caressed her tongue with his. Already he was steel hard. It didn't take much when he was touching her, seeing her in an intimate way that only her husband should.

Then he pulled free, as reluctantly as she did. Tears filled her eyes, and she quickly blinked them back. "We must hurry." Her voice was husky, and she hastily moved away from him.

This time she walked with confidence and he was convinced she felt comfortable about carrying the arrow. But he was disturbed by her distress and wished somehow he could make it right between them.

This time, *he* could barely walk, as aroused as he was.

***

When Aila arrived back at her chamber, she fully intended to remove the bundle herself, without anyone

74

else's help, but Alban had secured it so well, she had to ask her sister to untie it.

"You said you were going to speak with Inghean about taking care of the maids," Wynda accused.

"Aye. And we did."

"So what is this?"

"Something I must turn over to Alban. Do hurry. He is waiting and he will probably believe I am keeping it for myself."

"The arrow?" Wynda struggled to untie the knot. "How in the world did you get the knot this tight?"

"He wanted to make sure it didna slip..." Aila paused. Did she just say *he*?

Wynda's eyes couldn't get any rounder.

"Can you get it or no'?" Aila asked impatiently.

"Nay, I canna. I would have to cut it. But I would risk cutting you."

"Oh, just cut the pouch that he, uhm, I made and remove the arrow. We must examine it before we turn it over to Alban."

Wynda let out her breath and shook her head, then took her dirk and made a careful slice into the fabric, though Aila had planned to return the cloths to their rightful owners unscathed. When Wynda had removed the arrow, Aila dropped the hem of her kirtle, then the two of them examined the fletching, the feathers used to stabilize the arrow's flight, the shaft, and the arrowhead.

"The shaft doesna have a groove to knock the arrow," Aila observed.

"What? It has to have. How else could the arrow be nocked?" Wynda touched the end of the arrow that was shaped into a point just like the front of the arrow, instead of having a carved notch.

"That could be good for identifying the hunter, could it no'? How unusual to have a nockless arrow. 'Tis possible only one man would own such a weapon." Aila rubbed the knotted band around her waist. How in the world was she going to get it off?

"I agree. Hard wood was used for the upper part of the arrow, which means someone wealthier possessed it. And lighter wood at the tail end."

A knock at the door had them both jumping. Mai went to get it. "'Tis Alban."

"I am coming." Aila took the arrow pieces and the cloths from Wynda, all but the one secured around her waist for all time, she was afraid. She crossed the floor to the door and handed them to him, all bundled up. "I canna untie the knot. Neither can my sister. Why did you have to tie it so tightly?"

"To keep it secure."

"She canna cut it off without worrying the knife would slip."

"I will untie it."

"You willna!" Wynda said indignantly.

"Can you cover the lady up so I can just see the part of her that needs to be undone? Like we did before," he said as if reminding Aila how they had worked this before since it seemed she was in trouble with her sister for what had happened.

"Oh, aye, of course. Why didna I think of it?" Why hadn't he thought of it before! For that matter, why hadn't she?

Once her maid had wrapped her in a spare brat, she lifted her kirtle and Alban stepped into the room to untie the knot. Even he had difficulty doing so. But he finally freed it and she took a relieved breath. "Thank you. Take it with you, will you? And when you have a chance, return it to Inghean?"

"Of course. Thank you, my lady."

"The arrow doesna have a nock," Aila said.

"That is unusual. The only time I have seen that is when a lord returned from the Crusades and showed me all about it. The bowstring would have a small ring tied where the nock would normally be placed. Then the pointed end of the arrow would slip into the ring, be drawn back, and released. The Arabs used it as a means to prevent their enemies from retrieving their arrows and using them against them. Several rings would be tied onto a bowstring to ensure one would always be available," Alban said. "Without a ring, the arrow could not be used and the bow would be useless."

"Then we can find him easily. All we have to do—"

"All *I* have to do, my lady."

She let out her breath. "Aye, is determine who uses a ring on his bow."

"We will be going on a hunt in a few days. When we do, I can see who does."

So would Aila.

CHAPTER 7

Alban had their men watch for anyone who might be using a nockless arrow. They were also to listen to any conversations that might lead them to the conclusion that someone they knew had shot Sim.

So far, they hadn't learned anything and it had been four days now. Nothing untoward had happened to the king, and Sim was eager to get back to his work, so he returned to do his job, which meant whatever his superior asked of him.

They hoped no one would target him again. No one had seemed in the least bit interested in the man, so they assumed the hunter who had shot him either did so by accident, or was trying to shoot the king.

Alban had managed to stay away from Aila so she had a chance to court lords who might take an interest in her, but it was killing him to do so.

At the meal that night, Ward said, "What you are

TERRY SPEAR

doing is admirable."

Alban grunted. If the lass had not been of noble birth, he would have been the one to court her.

"Seriously," Ward said. "I have seen the way the two of you look at each other, moonstruck, and yet, you are trying your darnedest not to cause trouble. Ruining her chances of a match would do more harm than good if she could find a lord who is agreeable to her."

"So you say. It all depends on the match," Alban said morosely. The only match he liked the idea of was one where he was with the lady. Alban poked at his fish stew. "At least I dinna think the lady is querying anyone further about the incident." At least he hoped she was not. She hadn't spoken with him in days, so he assumed she hadn't learned anything more.

He watched as she talked with Lady Umberton again, seeming to have made a friend in her, and he was glad for that.

"You still show too much interest in her," Ward said. "I have had three lords enquire as to why you act like you have a chance with the lady."

"And you said?"

"Only that you worried about the lady because of her maids. And Lord Gustafson said you should dance with the servants outside and leave the ladies to the titled lords."

"Lord Gustafson, mayhap by the king's own orders, asked Lord Dunlap to dance with the lady," Alban said.

Ward nodded. "Aye. True enough. But that is what

the steward said."

Suddenly, Aila looked in Alban's direction and the way her lips were parted and her eyes wide, he wondered if she'd gotten some news that would help with the case. He was hopeful, but also concerned. He did not want her asking anything further about the situation!

Yet he was eager to learn what she knew.

"Now what?" Ward asked.

Alban turned to see what Ward was referring to, but his brother was watching Aila too. So he had seen the same thing as Alban had.

"Possibly something else and it has naught to do with the case."

"Or possibly she is asking questions again that will put her at risk." Ward sighed. "I wish you could marry the lady and take her well away from here so you could keep her out of harm's way."

"Aye, me too."

When the meal was ended, Aila and Wynda waited for everyone to leave the great hall, talking away to each other as if they were so engrossed in conversation, they didn't realize everyone was leaving. He and Ward also waited for the hall to clear out. But then he noticed five lords were watching Aila and her sister.

"Mayhap we should try to learn what we can later," Ward said, "when the ladies do not have as much of an audience."

Alban realized just how impatient he could be and

wanted to know now what Aila had learned. They had absolutely no evidence that anyone was attempting to assassinate the king, so they couldn't make accusations based on nothing.

Then the five lords approached the ladies, and Aila glanced back at Alban. He bowed his head a little in acknowledgement and then he and Ward left. Ward wanted to see to their men out in the field. But Alban wanted to go to their chamber and wait for word from Aila.

***

Aila couldn't wait to tell Alban who used a nockless arrow, according to Lady Umberton. The lady had been close enough to see him knock his arrow, and when he did, she saw the ring the pointed part of the back end of the arrow went into. She'd thought it was unusual, which was why she had noticed. The Earl of Dunlap was the owner of such an arrow.

And who approached to speak to Aila and her sister after the meal? None other than the lord himself. Also, Lord Comyn, Lord Farquharson, Lord Pierce, and Lord Tarleton.

Even Lady Umberton hung around, probably because she was interested in seeing what the gentlemen had to say to them. Maybe hoping one would be interested in her. Aila prayed the woman didn't reveal that she was asking about a nockless arrow.

Farquharson and Tarleton were clearly interested in Wynda. Both were talking to her exclusively. To Aila's

82

horror, Lady Umberton had to mention about the arrow and Aila's heart nearly stopped beating.

Wynda glanced in Aila's direction, despite having been engaged in speaking with the other gentlemen. But she'd heard the comment Lady Umberton had made, and looked to see if Aila was all right.

Aila was not all right. She felt lightheaded, like she could swoon. But she wasn't about to. She was certain she'd lost all the color in her cheeks. She just hoped Dunlap wouldn't notice.

"I am surprised you would have noticed the arrow, Lady Umberton," Dunlap said.

"Oh, well, it is quite unusual and while I watched you pull your bow back taut, I realized you had the oddest shaped arrow. I wouldna have known what it was called until Lady Aila enquired if anyone had used one that I had seen. And, of course, I thought of you."

Dunlap's dark gaze shifted to Aila. "You did? How would *you* know of such a thing?"

Aila wanted the floor to swallow her up. She couldn't say Alban had told her. If she did, she would make the lord aware he was also looking into who owned such an arrow.

"Our da," Aila quickly said.

Wynda agreed. "Aye. We just had never seen anyone else use one before."

"If so, why enquire now? Something must have caused you to ask," Dunlap said, putting her on the spot.

All the gentlemen were quiet now. Studying Aila.

Waiting. So was her sister, and Lady Umberton.

"I was curious what it would be like to use one," Aila quickly said, hoping she hadn't sounded like she had finally come up with a satisfactory reason and had blurted it out. "Our da wouldna allow us to use his. And no one else we have ever gone hunting with has had them. But there were so many people on the hunt today, I wondered if anyone else might have been using such unusual bows."

"So you asked Lady Umberton," Lord Dunlap asked.

"She is very observant and I thought she might have noticed when I had not."

Lady Umberton preened a bit at Aila's words.

Dunlap smirked. "Well, on the next hunt, you can use one of the rings from my bow and some of my arrows to try your hand at it. It takes some getting used to."

"Oh, I am delighted, to be sure. My thanks, my lord."

"My pleasure."

Her sister was looking at her like she was mad. But what else could Aila say? She couldn't think of another reason to get herself out of the bind she was in. She could just imagine what Alban would say. But at least she hadn't implicated him.

The gentlemen said they would see the ladies later for dancing, and Lady Umberton was pleased Lord Comyn and Lord Dunlap had asked her to dance later. When the gentlemen left, Lady Umberton fanned herself. "Oh my, it pays to visit with you ladies. And here all the others said it wouldna. I will see you later." She left with her maid, and Wynda pinned Aila with a glower.

Aila lifted her chin. "Dinna scold me. We now know who uses the arrows that wounded Sim."

"You are going to get yourself killed."

They left the great hall as the servants began to clear the trestle tables from the room.

"I willna. I will remain in sight of everyone. There are so many that are hunting, it willna be a problem," Aila said softly to her sister.

"Just as Sim was shot in front of many! Not only that, but you managed to get off alone before."

"That was different."

"How so? Did you lose your way? You never said how you ended up with Alban when you and he were listening to the men speaking in the woods."

Aila pulled her to a stop and whispered, "I saw a white... Oh, come on." She hurried her to their chamber and hadn't reached it when Alban stepped out of his.

Och, Alban would be furious with her. If she hadn't cared about him, she would have dismissed his concern at once. But she knew he cared about her as more than just a friend and he worried about her. Well, she worried about herself too.

She figured she would stay with a crowd of people at all times on the hunt and then nothing could go wrong.

"What did you learn?" Alban asked Aila, coming

straight to the point.

She folded her arms. "That Lord Dunlap has nockless arrows."

"And he is going to show her how to use them the next time we are on a hunt," Wynda said, looking at Alban with hopefulness as if he could save the day.

***

Aila knew Alban and his brother would watch her constantly on the hunt the next day. But tonight, she was stuck dancing with Lord Dunlap for the third time already. She desperately wanted to be with Alban, who looked like he was ready to go to battle, instead of enjoying the festivities. She knew as soon as she was done with the dance, he would be questioning her about everything Lord Dunlap had said.

"You are a most unusual young lady," Lord Dunlap said. "I wouldna think a woman such as yourself would be that interested in...arrows."

"Well, you never know when the knowledge could come in handy."

"Do you really want to try one of my arrows on the morrow?"

"Of course. I may no' be very good at it, but I would love to try."

"I knew your father. No' well. I dinna recall him using arrows like that."

Was he lying? She didn't remember ever having seen him before. But that didn't mean he hadn't seen her da somewhere else when she wasn't with him. "Lord

Dunlap, when you were on the hunt, were you no' shocked to see the king on foot when the boar charged him? Just hearing about it gives me shivers."

"Nay. I wasna there."

"You were no'?" Was he lying?

"Nay. When the king goes after his prey, no one else can. I wanted to hunt, so I went after another boar. Several of us did. Lord Farquharson and Tarleton were with me too."

"Oh. Then you didna witness the servant being accidentally shot."

"Nay. I am certain whoever shot the poor man was trying to protect the king and Sim got in the way. Sim was one of the men who were supposed to bring the meat back, but he got a little ahead of himself, trying to please the king, I suspect."

If Lord Dunlap hadn't shot the man, then who had? Someone else with nocked arrows?

"Is anyone else using nocked arrows here?"

Lord Dunlap looked askance at her. "Are you wanting someone else to show you how to shoot one?" He looked like he was teasing her, a little. But also curious as to why she was so interested in the arrows.

She smiled in her most amiable way. "Of course not. I look forward to you showing me how 'tis done." Especially *if* he hadn't been hatching any murderous plans. Not that she really cared to try it—well, yes, she did—but she had more important business to take care of then shooting arrows for fun.

***

That night alone in her bedchamber with Wynda, the maids sleeping on their pallets nearby, Aila had every intention of asking her sister if she'd check with Farquharson to see if Dunlap had been with him on the hunt. Then again, what if those two men were in on it. And Tarleton too? And they'd all covered for each other. Who was to say Dunlap wasn't just hidden in the woods and shot his arrow from there?

As soon as she asked Wynda, her sister let out her breath with exasperation. "It isna bad enough that you are questioning everyone to death about this matter, but you now want me to also?"

Aila turned on her side as she spoke with her sister. She needed her to understand she was not giving up on trying to learn the truth. "We need to know for certain, one way or another. What if Tarleton or Farquharson wants to marry you but they were involved in some kind of terrible plot? If Dunlap was truly with the other two men, and we can get someone else to verify it, then who else possesses arrows without nocks?"

"What if they want to know why I am asking? Or they tell Lord Dunlap that I was inquiring about this?" Wynda pulled her covers over her shoulder.

"You can make it sound as though you're curious about...well, who took the boar down first? That way you are not asking if he was there with the others. You could even say that he raced past Alban to get the last boar of the hunt, and you wondered if he had missed out on the one he and the others had targeted. If one of the men says he wasna with them, then we have our answer." It seemed simple enough to Aila.

"All right. That should sound innocent enough." Wynda rolled a curl of hair around her fingers.

"I suppose you canna just come out and ask them if anyone else uses a nockless arrow," Aila added.

"Nay."

Still, Aila knew there had to be a way to discuss it that wouldn't put them in harm's way. "What if you say something about how your sister is fascinated in Lord Dunlap's nockless arrows and wonders if anyone else uses such a thing. She becomes obsessed with the oddest things at times. Then see if he knows anyone else who might have them."

"Our da?"

"What? He never...oh, aye, we said he did. Agreed, but then all you need to say is he would never let us use them and he said no one did. So that made me curious." Aila thought it sounded reasonable.

"If I can mention it without getting myself into trouble, I will. Otherwise, I willna. I saw that Alban spoke with you briefly."

She ran her hand over the covers. "Aye. He is angry with me this time. I think he was trying to make a fuss over what I had talked to Dunlap about so he could impress upon me that I shouldna speak to anyone else about such matters."

"Well, he is right."

"Mayhap there is naught to this. If so, then no one should care about my inquiries." Aila hoped that was truly the case.

"But if there is?"

"Then mayhap we will be the heroines of the day." Aila smiled at her sister, thinking what a noble thing that would be.

"Or dead," Wynda said, reminding her of just how dangerous this could be.

CHAPTER 8

"Since naught more has happened concerning the shooting incident, I would like to believe it was just an accident." Alban couldn't keep his eyes off Aila any more than usual while they broke their fast that morn. They were hunting again today. He suspected no one would make an attempt on the king's life, if that was the case the last time, with nockless arrows or otherwise.

"Lady Aila had been quiet today, keeping to herself. Her sister doesna look happy either." Ward broke off a piece of bread and devoured it.

"I have noticed. Lady Umberton is sitting by a lord this morn, mayhap having caught his eye. Now, Lady Felicia is seated beside Lady Aila and I dinna think the two women get along."

"Unless 'tis necessary, dinna speak with the lady today. I fear you are being watched," Ward said.

"Lord Gustafson? Let him observe. I was invited

here. If the king wishes me gone, so be it."

Ward glanced at Alban.

Alban finished his bread. "All right. 'Tis true I dinna want to leave here, just yet. No' while I am concerned about a particular woman's safety. You know she is riding alongside Lord Dunlap at the hunt?"

"Aye. She is a lady. He is a lord. Mayhap they will be a match."

"Mayhap he wishes something else of her."

"Which is why you should be careful of speaking with her, but we will both be observing the two of them the whole time we are on the hunt."

"Aye." Alban wasn't happy about it, but he didn't have a choice.

As soon as the meal was done, they rose and waited for the king and queen to depart, and then Ward and Alban watched as Lord Dunlap joined Aila. Alban had never cared at all about anything that had to do with being titled, except when it came to Aila. Though he reminded himself that even if he were, that wouldn't guarantee that he could obtain her hand in marriage. It still depended on the king's whim.

He was sure if Lord Dunlap wanted the lady's hand, the king would give it. Maybe she was even considering such a thing, if she learned he wasn't involved in any nefarious plan to harm anyone.

With that thought in mind, he and Ward followed the rest of the courtiers and guests out and he intended to guard Aila's back as much as he could.

"Dinna be so conspicuous about it," Ward warned him.

Alban shook his head, but if the lord needed reminding that he and the lady were being observed, mayhap he would take greater care with her.

***

Aila hoped Alban was watching out for her, but she couldn't keep looking around to see if he was, as much as she wanted to. She just had to take it on faith that he was.

As soon as they were out in the woods, Lord Dunlap stopped his horse and dismounted. Then he helped her down from her horse. She shouldn't have worried if Alban was watching. Nearly a dozen paused to see what they were up to. Or maybe not. Maybe they had already heard that she intended to try a nockless arrow today and wanted to see how miserably she did. The king and the rest of the hunters were off on the hunt so she was surprised so many others were interested in what she was doing with Dunlap.

"Aim at that tree, just in case anyone is moving in that direction beyond our sight."

That had her truly concerned. What if she missed the tree—with a regular arrow, she couldn't, but with this one, she wasn't certain—and injured or killed someone? What if she hit the king?

"Mayhap we should try this on a target back at the keep," she said, wishing she'd thought of that before.

Several people snickered. She didn't care what they

thought or if they believed she was afraid. She didn't want to accidentally hurt anyone.

Lord Dunlap showed her how to use the arrow in the ring, pulled the string taught, and loosed it. It hit the tree right in the center.

For an instant, she thought what had the tree ever done to him? Then he handed her the bow and the nockless arrow. And he stood behind her and showed her how to pull the string taut. She knew that part. And she was way too close for comfort. If Alban had held her in such an intimate manner, she would have loved it. Probably turned in his arms and kissed him. But with Lord Dunlap, she didn't feel like melting into the woodland floor. She wanted to duck out from beneath his grasp.

Everyone was deadly silent. Maybe because they didn't want to ruin her concentration. Or maybe because they were intrigued with the lord's actions.

Now she wished Alban wasn't here to see this.

She pulled the string taut and let it loose. It struck the tree right above Lord Dunlap's arrow. He smiled down at her. "Well done."

Everyone in the audience clapped. "She can go with me on the hunt any day," a lord said whom she didn't know.

She noticed Gustafson was watching too. He didn't seem pleased. But then again, he never seemed pleased with anything that she did or didn't do.

To her surprise, Lady Felicia asked, "Can you show

me too?"

But Lord Dunlap just shook his head. "We are here to hunt for the meal. Mayhap later we can have target practice, like Lady Aila mentioned."

The woman smiled sweetly, but she cast Aila a cutting look.

Then everyone was off to the hunt, though Lord Dunlap stayed with Aila for a time. She was surprised, knowing how important the hunt was to him. "You are good with the bow," he said to her.

"You were an excellent teacher." She had to say it. Her mother taught her to be a gentle lady, when she wasn't kissing a Highlander outside his chamber, or trying to chase down evil men.

She had hoped the lord would soon get the urge to chase after a boar, and when he finally did, saying he hoped to have the pleasure of dining with her—which completely shocked her—he took off, and she breathed a sigh of relief.

"You are excellent with the bow, my lady," Alban said. "Most likely any kind of arrow, I might add."

"I thank you for saying so." She smiled up at him.

"Well?"

"I dinna know if he has anything to do with anything. Wynda is asking if he was with a couple of lords during the other hunt when he said he had helped to take down a boar."

Alban shook his head. "Lady Aila—"

"She is being careful. We have it all worked out."

"Somehow that doesna lessen my concern. You are dining with the earl tonight."

"Aye. 'Tis no' my choice, mind you," she told him, as they had found themselves quite alone. "Tomorrow the king is having the boat races. Will you and your brother come with Wynda and me?"

"I would, but the king's steward has already told me that we willna be rowing with any of the eligible ladies. We can follow after the boats make the halfway mark. My brother and I will try our best to catch up to you."

She smiled. "I have no doubt you will make it and pass us by even."

"I would, to prove to the lords who accompany you that they are no' as capable we are. But in reality, I would stay close by, watching over the situation, just in case."

"Do you realize we are alone in the woods again?"

"Which is the only reason we are able to have this discussion. I wonder if you are able to use a regular arrow as well as you are the nockless one, or if Lord Dunlap's assistance made a difference." Alban couldn't help wanting to be the one who did the honor this time.

"Well, there is only one way to find out." She dismounted on her own. "Hand me your bow and arrow, sir, and we shall see."

Glad she was willing to accept the challenge, he dismounted, but when he handed her the bow, he also took her hand and pulled her into his arms. "Could you use *my* instruction? You dinna know how much it killed me to be watching Dunlap holding you close to show you how to shoot the arrow."

"If you think I need the instruction."

"I doubt you do." But he wanted to hold her close like Dunlap had, to feel her body against his, to cherish the moment for as long as he was able. Somehow they managed to shoot the arrow, but in the next instant she had turned in his arms, dropped the bow, and was kissing him like she'd never be able to kiss him again. In truth, he feared that was so. He shouldn't compromise her like this. Yet when it came to Aila, he had no willpower.

He brushed his hands over her breasts, wanting her, all of her.

"Ahem," someone said, and both whipped around to see Ward watching them. "Lady Wynda was concerned that her sister had fallen behind and couldna keep up. But I see my brother found you."

"No' another word." Alban helped Aila onto her horse.

"Another lesson in archery?" Ward asked, looking at Alban's arrow in the tree. "'Tis impressive. I might have to try that maneuver with the lasses."

"Lady Felicia is looking for an instructor," Aila said.

"Aye, but I dare say she is interested in Lord Dunlap instructing her and no' anyone else. Besides, it wouldna do to fall for a lady when I could never court her."

Alban knew his brother was not being mean-hearted, that he only worried about Alban's continued interest in Aila. His brother was right, as much as Alban didn't want to acknowledge it.

Raleen and Mai, the ladies' maids, suddenly joined them. "Lady Wynda told us to join you and stay with you," Raleen said.

"And what about my sister being without a maid?" Aila asked.

"She is with several ladies right now. But she did want to speak with you about some news."

"Take me to her at once." Not that Wynda could reveal the news to Aila when others were within hearing, unless she could tell her in a secret way. But even a shake of her head could mean...well, she wasn't sure. No, Dunlap hadn't been with the men on the hunt? No, he hadn't been near the king at the time?

They soon caught up with her sister, others scattering to hunt stag and boar.

"Lord Farquharson was telling me how he got the first shot at the boar they took down the other day. Lord Tarleton after him. Lord Dunlap didna show up until it was too late. But then he heard Alban shouting and headed that way for a chance to take down the last of the boars needed for the meals."

Aila frowned. "Late, eh?"

"Aye. I said I was surprised he was late, given his interest in hunting."

Ward and Alban exchanged glances.

"Lord Dunlap said something had come up and he would join them right afterwards, to not finish off the boar until he could help. Of course, they couldna hold off. It wouldna have been humane to the boar and if the lord had other pressing matters to attend to, whoever showed up, it was their game. I had to agree with Lord Farquharson."

"What about the—"

"No one has any." Wynda gave her sister a look that said do not speak of the arrows out loud.

"Oh. Lord Dunlap wished me to sit beside him at the meal tonight." Aila didn't sound happy about it.

Alban hoped she wasn't going to ask Lord Dunlap what important business he had to conduct, which made him miss hunting the boar with his lordly friends when he'd already said he'd gone to hunt with them.

***

Alban was giving Aila pointed looks across the great hall that evening. She knew he was concerned that she would speak about what business Lord Dunlap had been dealing with that made him miss hunting with his friends. She wasn't that naïve. If it meant he'd tried to kill the king in that time, and she let on she knew about it, she could be at real risk.

Besides, she had other problems. Lord Comyn had mentioned to Lord Gustafson that she had been alone with a Highland commoner on the hunt, and he wanted Gustafson to tell the king.

Thankfully, Gustafson had told the lord, and her, that the king was more concerned with other matters, and, in fact, he and a maid had been nearby.

Which had nearly stopped her heart. Had he been nearby? Had he overheard what they'd been discussing? And seen her kissing Alban, and him running his hands over her breasts, making her hot and intrigued?

She didn't think so. She thought he was trying to keep the news from angering the king. Which, from what she understood, he was very good at doing—if the news wasn't such that he felt the king needed to hear it. But she worried Ward had seen Alban and her kissing too. And the rest.

"I am curious about some things concerning the hunt, my lady," Lord Dunlap said, and all of a sudden, Aila felt chilled. "Your sister was talking to Lord Farquharson concerning my absence for a few minutes before I joined them on the hunt, and then there is this business with the arrow. I am certain you have something you would like for me to explain further. I would like very much to do so. I believe men and women should discuss topics that they have on their minds. No sense in trying to second guess when we can be perfectly honest with one another."

"I wholeheartedly agree." But there was no way she was going to ask him what he'd been doing that had delayed him from arriving in time to hunt the boar with his friends. If he had indeed shot Sim, he wasn't going to tell her the truth anyway. So instead, she asked, "You are so right. And I wanted to ask you why you hunt with the nockless arrow."

Lord Dunlap cast her a small smile. He was not

witless. He knew she wanted to know more than that, but since she didn't ask, he told her all about the Arab who had taught him about nockless arrows and the reason for them. Which she already knew.

"You will dance with me this eve, will you no'?" he asked.

"Aye, of course." She smiled sweetly at him. Could he be the devil himself?

"I did want to mention I have heard the most alarming news concerning you and Alban, however."

She tried not to stiffen at hearing his words. "Oh?"

"You know how gossip is. Lady Felicia tells a group of women, Lord Comyn overhears, he mentions it to the king's steward..."

"Alban has been helpful to my sister and me when we needed someone's assistance in rousing the healer from her pallet to take care of our sick maids. He was very kind in doing so. As to the dances"—she lifted her chin—"no one asked me to dance and he was being nice to offer."

"Both heroic endeavors, I agree. People will say what they wish because it makes them feel more important. But when I choose a wife, I want to know that she doesna have feelings for some other man. Nor has she acted on those emotions."

She wanted to tell him she had kissed Alban, and if that ruined her chances with him or any other lord here, so be it. She would take the way she felt about him to the grave, but she would never have wished to have done anything differently.

She smiled. "Lady Felicia wants you to marry her. She is upset with me for any attentions you cast my way. If we are being perfectly honest with one another, I have never lain with a man, any man. Just so you know." Normally, she wouldn't have told any man that, but she respected Lord Dunlap—if he was not an attempted murderer—for bringing the gossip to her attention. He could have just kept it to himself and thought the worst of her.

Although *if* he'd seen the way Alban had kissed her and she had wantonly kissed him back, he might have believed Felicia's claim.

"Lord Comyn is always looking for a way to garner some favor from the king, so he feels if he passes the gossip along, no matter whether any of it is true or not, that will earn him some favor," Lord Dunlap said. "Thankfully, Lord Gustafson is good about not giving into the gossip unless he learns 'tis completely factual and can be substantiated."

She was glad for that, though she imagined Gustafson suspected plenty where she and Alban were concerned. After they concluded the meal, Lord Dunlap wanted to walk with her, and so she was unable to speak with Alban, or her sister, before the dance began. But she was afraid that either he was keeping her close because she knew too much and he wanted to learn just how much, or he was really interested in her as a marriage prospect. After the way she had seen him treat

Alban on the hunt, nearly knocking him from his horse, she wasn't interested in the earl in the least bit. But she wasn't sure she'd have any say in the matter anyhow. Still, she could always tell him she'd lost her heart to Alban, if Dunlap truly wanted to wed her, and that would be the end of that.

When she retired to bed that night, her sister said, "The gossip all over court is that Lord Dunlap is planning to marry you." But Wynda didn't look happy for her. More concerned instead.

"I still dinna know if he wanted to do anything bad to anyone," Aila said, as the maids helped them out of their clothes.

"But you love another."

Aila took a deep breath and nodded.

"What will you do if he asks the king for your hand in marriage?"

"I will tell him I love another. And hope that he will understand. Tomorrow the boat races commence. I was so hoping we could go with Alban and Ward."

"Aye, I know. We willna know until tomorrow as to who will be with whom. Though I have it on good authority that you and I will be in the same boat with whoever the gentlemen are."

Aila smiled. "At least that will be good." She told her about Lord Dunlap's comments concerning the hunt.

Wynda didn't say anything as they slipped under the covers. "So he believes you suspect something then."

"Aye."

"If I could, I would say something to hurt Felicia's reputation for casting disparaging remarks about your character," Wynda said.

"We are above being gossips." But then she smiled at Wynda. "Unless of course we can learn something that is true."

CHAPTER 9

Alban and his brother watched as the last of the boats disappeared around the peninsula of the loch. "Come on. Let us go take care of this business, and then come back to see who wins, but I canna say I like that Lord Comyn was one of the men in the boat, not after he was so condescending concerning Aila."

"Mayhap Gustafson planned it that way, to allow her a say in the situation."

Alban snorted. "Even if the lady did have her say, I doubt Lord Comyn will believe anything but what he wants to believe. Which is the worst in people."

"Have you ever noticed that people like that can sometimes be the least trustworthy because they have something to hide?"

"Aye, true enough." Alban knew Aila would be miserable. At least she had her sister as a companion.

He and his brother were headed back to their camp

to speak with their men. They'd had word that some of their clansmen's discussions with other clansmen might have given them a lead. Often when men wouldn't talk to the brothers, they would feel freer to talk to their guardsmen about issues. Women, duties, battles they fought in, and more—like who might have been interested in the arrow that had wounded Sim.

But Alban was surprised to see Sim speaking to their men, gesticulating wildly, motioning to another man that Alban's clansmen were holding in place. He was a short, tawny-haired fellow, with shifty eyes, and he did indeed look guilty about something, though he was shaking his head and clearly denying whatever it was.

Everyone turned to see Alban and his brother riding into camp and Sim pointed to the man. "He is the one! He is Lord Comyn's man. He wanted the arrow that shot me. Indeed, he was the one who shot it!"

"You are sure? You said naught about this before," Alban reminded him.

"Aye. Before I was attempting to keep away from the boar, I had been trying to recall who all was there. If someone had been trying to kill the king, then you needed to know. Lord Comyn was there and his man. This man. He was holding a bow for Lord Comyn and so was the lord himself. I thought it odd that he was ready to shoot two bows. But something glinted off the one Lord Comyn was holding. A ring, the sunlight shining on it for a moment. That was what had distracted me when the boar came after me, I realized. My friend shouted for me to run. I turned quickly and saw the king on foot near me. We were both in the path of the angry boar. Then I was shot. I didn't think anything of it until later when I began running the whole scene through my mind.

"I asked Lord Comyn's man when he started to use nockless arrows. He said he never had and was all growly about it. Said I had better mind my own business or else. Well, then I knew Lord Comyn had shot me and this bastard was lying about it. One of my friends was told to carry water to Lord Comyn's chamber. He wasna there, and she brought the bow with the ring on it to me."

"I told him Lord Comyn doesna use such a bow," the man said. "Someone must have planted it there. Lord Dunlap's man. The lord is the only one who uses such a bow."

"Except Lord Dunlap's bows, the three he has in his chamber, have a carving of a stag's head. Why would he have that on three of his bows and not the fourth? And why would he frame Lord Comyn when the baron doesna even use such a weapon?"

One of Alban's clansmen showed the bow to Alban, then he passed it on to Ward.

"The servant said 'tis made in the same wood, has the same grain, and the symbol of a falcon on each. Lord Comyn's symbol. She found six nockless arrows hidden beneath the bed in Lord Comyn's chamber."

"'Tis all we needed to know. Bring the men, the bows, and the arrows," Ward said to their men. "We must take this information to the king at once."

"Lady Aila and Wynda," Alban said, and rode off, his heart thundering.

"Gustafson is with them." Ward galloped after Alban.

"Aye, and what if Gustafson was behind all of this?" Alban had never figured the king's steward would be in on any of this.

"They wouldna do any harm to the women."

"Why would they plan to take them out in the boat? Those two men? Who always scheduled everything? Gustafson. He knew where everyone would be. He was the one who used the king's name to order everyone about." Alban didn't think this was just by chance.

"But he didna tell the king the ugly rumors Lady Felicia and Lord Comyn were spreading concerning Lady Aila."

"Mayhap because he didna want the king to be aware of it. The more he told him about her, the more the king would be thinking about what to do with her. If she was of no consequence, just another lady amidst a castle of courtiers, if she died, he wouldna think on it for long. We must hurry and stop their boat if we can." Alban didn't want to believe the women could be in harm's way when he couldn't reach them easily to rescue them.

"As much time as has gone by, they should nearly be to the halfway point by now," Ward warned.

"Then we shall ride like the wind."

***

The afternoon was sunny and warmer than the past week and today, just perfect for the boat races. Two gentlemen and two ladies were in each of the boats. Supposedly, the ladies' suitors were to be paired up with them. Aila knew she didn't have a suitor and the couple of lords who had appeared interested in Wynda hadn't joined them at their boat either. Rather, Lord Comyn and the king's steward did.

Lord Comyn must have been told he had to go with them. Aila imagined Lord Gustafson took it upon himself to make the correct number of pairings before someone like Alban interceded.

Aila so wished he could have come with them instead. They would have had so much more fun. Both brothers were watching from the shore, along with a number of guests and staff. The whole point of the exercise was to have the courting couples participate together. So though she had looked forward to doing this with her sister, she had not looked forward to who might boat with them. Especially when Lord Comyn was the one who had helped to spread the rumors about her and Alban, this was going to be even more uncomfortable for her. Her sister gave a knowing look like she would rather push him overboard for what he'd said about Aila, than ride with him in the boat.

Lord Comyn looked sour, probably because he hadn't wanted to be with them any more than they wanted him to be here. Gustafson was chatting more than usual, talking about the weather and tomorrow's feast, about another hunt where the woman could take their falcons.

But when they reached the middle of the loch, Lord Comyn stopped rowing. It was supposed to be a race. Aila felt uneasy. She couldn't say why exactly, except she knew Comyn didn't like her. And Gustafson had not been really happy with her either.

"We will lose the race," she cheerfully said. "Mayhap you are tired and Wynda and I can row for a while." She'd noted all the boats had gotten so far ahead of them, they were no longer visible and she couldn't imagine as good a shape as Comyn was in, that he couldn't row any faster than this.

"We have a rather unusual problem," Gustafson said.

Aila feared the worst. Were these the two men she and Alban had heard talking in the woods that day, plotting a murder? This was so not good. And her sister was right in the middle of it when she shouldn't have been.

"We are curious about your interest in the man who was shot accidentally during the hunt," Gustafson said.

"Oh, aye, well, I do believe the lord who shot him should have apologized to the poor man. I dinna believe 'tis good manners to treat a servant thusly, and act as though it was his fault for getting in the way of the boar." She prayed the lords believed her.

Her sister was sitting like a statue, though Aila noticed Wynda glance behind them. Others who were not looking for marriages would be rowing boats later. She hoped some of them would show up and save them if they needed their aid. She realized Gustafson must have planned this all along as they were right in the middle of the loch, too far from any shore to swim to easily, unable to see anyone because of the way two peninsulas jutted out, one hiding the shore they'd come from and one hiding the one ahead, so they were quite out of sight.

She was afraid Gustafson had already made up his mind that she knew they were the ones behind the assassination attempt. How she wished they *had* known and could have let the king know! But without substantial proof, she also realized neither she nor Alban would have been able to sway the king's opinion concerning two of his most loyal subjects.

"So that is why you asked Lady Umberton about who had shot the servant."

"Aye."

"And you learned?" Gustafson asked as the boat sat idly in the water, a breeze stirring, causing the boat to rock a little.

If she could grab one of the oars and hit Gustafson with it, she would. She wished she could tell her sister to grab the other oar and whack Comyn on the head. Except Aila feared neither might be successful, and they might have a better chance to just jump overboard before the lords used the oars on them.

"Well, only Lord Dunlap had the kind of arrow that

shot Sim. So naturally, I knew it had to be him."

"And you told him he should apologize to the servant."

"Aye. And you know what he said? Well, he said he wasna even there. Which couldna have been the truth. So I asked him if he had witnesses to say he was somewhere else at the time. And do you know what he said?" Aila folded her arms, looking as indignant as she could.

"Pray tell, my lady, what did he say?" Gustafson wasn't amused. He seemed annoyed.

"Well, he said he had been hunting with Lords Tarleton and Farquharson. But when we asked them, they said he was late in coming and missed the boar hunt completely! Which goes to prove my point."

"Which is?" Lord Comyn asked.

"Why that he accidentally shot Sim, and then was too arrogant to admit it. And then he missed taking down the boar with Tarleton and the other lord. Lord Dunlap was so bound and determined to get the last boar of the hunt—that I had found and Alban was chasing--that Dunlap nearly unseated Alban from his horse. On *purpose*! The nerve of the man. So I ask you, what kind of a lord acts in such a way?"

"Someone who is attempting to assassinate the king but wounded the servant instead?" Gustafson asked.

Aila felt lightheaded all at once because she hadn't expected him to come out with those words exactly and so she thought she must have paled and looked as distressed as she felt, which should work in her favor. "Nay. Are...you positive? Why has he no' been arrested?"

"Someone took the arrow that was used on Sim."

She didn't know what to say. Did he know Alban had it? Did he know the part that Alban had taken in all of this?

"That would have proven what? That he had shot the servant, but had naught to do with attempting to kill the king."

"But you think someone is plotting to kill the king. Why?" Gustafson asked.

What had he heard?

"I know naught of any such plot. Without hesitation, I would have come to you about it, being that you are his loyal steward."

"Your questioning Lady Umberton, Inghean, and Lord Dunlap have started rumors that someone had attempted to assassinate the king."

"Lord Dunlap," she breathed out, figuring he had nothing to do with it, but if she pretended to believe so, maybe she and her sister would be safely taken to shore. But she was afraid that would not be the case. That Gustafson wanted to know exactly what she knew, and who else also had this knowledge. And then he planned to kill each and every one of them. If he planned to kill the king, then anyone else who got in his way would be incidental. In fact, he would probably just say they were all in on the conspiracy.

"Somehow you knew there was more to it than

that. How did you know?" Gustafson said.

She thought if they could talk about this long enough, surely someone would come around the treed peninsula and see them and then Gustafson and Comyn couldn't murder them.

"'Tis as I said. I believe Lord Dunlap should apologize to Sim, but if there is more at stake, then he should pay for his crime, by all means. I shudder to think of what could have happened to me if he realized that I thought he had planned to kill the king."

Gustafson smiled. "Very well. Lord Comyn was certain someone overheard us speaking in the woods. Then we saw you and Alban coming out of them together, alone. Then you began questioning the ladies about who had seen Sim get shot. You hadna even been there. So how did you learn of it, and why were you really so interested? Then you learned the king was on foot. And the concern grew. Care to change your story?"

Aila didn't breathe a word. She was afraid Gustafson and Comyn guessed they had eavesdropped, even though they hadn't actually witnessed them doing so. But now they knew for certain, and it was too late for her and her sister to get out of this dangerous predicament they found themselves in.

"So you tried to kill the king," Aila finally said. No reason to keep quiet about it now. They looked at Lord Comyn to see if he wouldn't talk this madman out of what he planned to do, but he only pulled out his dirk and motioned to them to get on with it. He was involved all the way, but she still had hoped he would see reason.

"So you were involved too." She despised the two of them, but she was scared for her sister for she wouldn't have had any part in it if Aila hadn't meddled so.

"Jump overboard, now," Gustafson said, murder in his black eyes.

Aila reached over and squeezed her sister's hand, then grabbed for one of the oars. She managed to grasp it before either of the men could react. She swung it at Gustafson's head and yelled at her sister, "Go." She struck him as hard as she could manage before he could respond. He cried out an oath before she tossed the oar into the loch, rocking the boat as she scrambled about.

Comyn moved to stick her with the dagger, and Aila screamed as loud as she could, "They are trying to kill us!" She had no hope that anyone would hear her from this far away, but she had to make the effort no matter what.

Then she dove into the water. The shock of the cold water hit her face and hands first, her brat water repellent for a bit. But eventually it would soak up the water.

"What are you doing! Have you both gone mad?" Gustafson shouted, as if to pretend the ladies just jumped overboard because they were foolish. "Let us help you!"

But Comyn was swearing up a storm as he tried to reach the other oar in the water and he was paddling away from her, trying to get to it as the currents moved the boat in the opposite direction.

Both she and Wynda were strong swimmers, but they were so far from any other boats and so far from land, she feared the men would try to hit them with their oars when they realized the women could swim.

"Go back the way we came," Aila told Wynda.

"We must stay together."

"Nay. They are coming after us, surely thinking they can kill us and then claim we drowned. If we are together, they can try to kill both of us at the same time. If we split up, we have a better chance of one of us making it."

Wynda's eyes filled with tears.

"Go, Wynda. Head for where some of the spectators may be milling about. Some more will be headed for the other side of the loch and could be just on the other side of the peninsula even now. You will surely catch up with some of them coming from that direction. Go!" And then with a heavy heart, Aila swam away from her sister, praying she would make it. Wynda had always been the slower swimmer of the two, and Aila had to give her a better chance at surviving.

Aila paused in the water, watching to see which way Gustafson would row the boat. He was heading toward Wynda. Probably because Wynda was making some headway toward the beginning point of their race. They might have thought Aila was treading water because she couldn't swim that far. This wouldn't do at all! She had to give her more of a head-start.

Aila shouted as she moved her legs and arms and treaded the cold water. "Gustafson and Lord Comyn tried to murder the king! Help us! They are trying to drown us!" She still didn't believe anyone would hear her from this point in the water. But when she saw him turn the boat in her direction, she began to swim toward shore again. Every so often, she'd cast a look back to make sure they were coming after her so that her sister had a chance to reach the other shore.

Even though they were good swimmers, Aila realized she'd never worn this many clothes to swim in. The wet brat was weighing her down too much. As much as she hated removing it and being even colder, she was afraid that unless she did, she'd never make it to shore at all. She fumbled with the brooch pinning it together. And finally managed to unfasten it, kicking her legs, trying to stay afloat.

She heard the boat growing closer, the hull hitting the ripples, the oars splashing.

Without the brat, she could swim a little faster. But her kirtle was nearly as heavy. She could do this, she told herself. She had to do this. She struggled to pull off her kirtle, not wanting to even think about how she would look when she arrived on the shore in just a sopping wet, nearly sheer chemise. But if losing her other garments meant the difference between escaping or death, she had no choice.

She imagined racing her sister across the loch and winning a prize—the only prize she wished to win with all her heart. *Alban.* In her dreams. But if she were to win, he would be her prize. She imagined him wrapping her in his plaid and holding her close, kissing her, and embracing her, so glad she had survived this treachery. And the thought of his concern for her brought tears to her eyes.

Which was not good. She had to be strong for her sister. If they caught up to Aila, they'd go after her sister next.

She heard her sister shouting off in the distance, and Aila turned to look, fearing Gustafson had maneuvered his boat around and had headed in her direction again. But he hadn't. He was too close to Aila now. Much too close.

Was her sister shouting for help for them both then? Or trying to distract the men like Aila had done?

Aila again swam off.

She hoped the men on the shore Wynda was trying to reach were going to her aid. Gustafson couldn't hope to get away with his plan. She wanted to tell them they should make a run for it while they still could. Not that she wanted them to get away with it. She would have a difficult enough time just reaching the shore, and not dying of a chill, she realized. She wasn't sure she could fend off these men if they tried to kill her from the boat or if she reached the shore and so did they.

The oars splashed steadily in the water. The boat slapped against the breeze-stirred ripples in the loch. Closer. Too close. And then she turned as Gustafson struck at her with his oar. She dove under the water, toward the boat, not away from it. In so doing, she touched the bottom and swam underneath the hull, until she was on the other side and came up for air. How she wished she could capsize the boat. Especially if the men could not swim.

She clung close to the side as they must have been facing the other way, not believing she could have dived under the boat.

"Do you see her?" Gustafson asked.

"Nay. You must have struck her hard enough that you killed her. Come, let us go after the other one before she makes it to shore and tells what has happened."

"Nay. Boats are surely headed her way," Gustafson growled.

"They might still have a long way to go."

"If we were to reach her in time, they would be too close by then and see what we were up to. 'Tis too late."

"So what are we doing now? We must make our escape."

"I canna believe two women have upset all our planning." Gustafson sat back down in the boat, and began dipping the oars into the water, only this time the boat headed for the shore.

Which made sense. They couldn't go back, nor could they go to the other side of the loch where everyone was finishing the boat races. And this was the closest side now to go to. But she couldn't swim in any other direction either. She wouldn't have the strength to fight the cold much longer. She hoped anyone else who might be rowing across the loch, not part of the race, would reach her sister quickly and pull her from the water. And somehow they'd get word to send men to save Aila.

CHAPTER 10

Alban and his brother rode their horses around the loch to reach the landing point at the finish line for the boats. Their men hadn't caught up to them yet. But when Alban and Ward heard a woman shouting from one of the peninsulas, he and Ward made their way through the trees and found a soaking wet Lady Wynda.

"God's wounds." Ward leapt from his saddle and removed his brat to cover Wynda.

"Aila," she sobbed, her skin blue. "Find her. Comyn and Gustafson were after her. She went to the east shore." She motioned in the direction, her words chilled as she tried to get them out. "Save her. Lord Comyn and Gustafson meant to kill us. They meant to kill the king."

"Stay with the lady," Alban said. "I will go after Aila."

He prayed he was not too late. But he remained focused. Find Aila. Save Aila. Kill Comyn and Gustafson.

***

"Aila!" Alban shouted.

Aila could barely swim toward shore she was so cold now. She couldn't believe he was truly coming for her. Had the others found her sister? Had she told them where Aila was? She wanted desperately to let Alban know where she was, but she couldn't shout back, fearful Gustafson would return to finish her off. The boat was getting closer to the beach now. She still had a ways to swim.

She continued to paddle as quietly as she could, willing herself to reach the shore. As long as they didn't realize she was following them, and as long as they abandoned the boat and then ran off, she could make it.

"Aila!" Alban yelled out again, desperation in his voice.

God, how she wanted to be with him, not just now, but forever. He must be coming from land, not on a boat. She had to reach the shore. To reach him. To warn him.

***

Alban couldn't lose Aila even though he knew he could never have her. He couldn't believe Lord Comyn and Gustafson were involved in the assassination attempt on the king when everything had pointed to Dunlap. Which must have been their plan. He was glad they had not gone to see the king with word that they believed Dunlap had tried to kill him.

"Aila!" Alban shouted. He knew he would alert Gustafson and Comyn that he was coming and he would risk all to save her life. If it meant they would face him and leave her alone, if she was still alive, he was willing to gamble on it.

"Aila!" Alban shouted. He feared the worst. But then, if she was still in the water, still trying to make it to shore, she wouldn't want to alert the men she was alive.

Then he saw movement in the woods near the water's edge. Aila? But Aila would have seen him. A boat ground against the shore, and he came through the trees to see the two men beach their boat and begin to get out. Alban whipped his bow up, nocked an arrow, and let it loose, striking Lord Comyn in the leg. He cried out and stumbled off. Alban quickly readied another arrow, but Gustafson ducked into shrubs near the water's edge and the arrow went into the water.

"Bastard," Alban ground out. Then he called out, "Aila!"

And then he saw her. She was nearly to shore, barely able to swim. If Gustafson hadn't run off, he could still grab Aila and use her as a hostage. Alban galloped his horse to the place where she'd made it to land, but she hadn't even crawled out of the water.

Alban jumped from his horse and dashed into the shallow water. He reached down and pulled Aila out of the loch and into his arms.

"Aila," he said, holding her tight, kissing the top of her head, feeling her trembling.

"I love you," she said, her words soft and breathless and shivery. "I won."

He worried about her state of mind then, but quickly set her down on the beach and crouching next to her, he hurried to pull off his plaid to wrap her in it. "Gustafson is nearby if he hasna left the area. Our men are on their way with the news about the murderous lords."

She clung to his shirt as if she was afraid he was going to leave her.

"I must remove your chemise as wet as it is. You will be warmer in my plaid without it." Then he helped her to stand and slipped it over her head. As soon as he had wrapped her in his plaid, Gustafson made a dash for Alban's horse.

Alban let go of Aila, yanked out his sword, and rushed at Gustafson, who stopped to unsheathe his sword. Shouts in the woods from some of his men verified they'd caught up with Lord Comyn. But for now, Alban's concentration was on Gustafson.

"You kill me and the king will have your head." Gustafson couldn't be serious.

Then again, maybe the king would want to do the honors. "Drop your sword and you can let the king decide your fate."

But Gustafson slashed at Alban, still wanting his horse, Alban presumed. It would be the only way he could manage to escape. A man on foot would never make it unless he had friends who were waiting somewhere to help him leave. Alban suspected he would, but that they were waiting for him to resolve the issue with the king first. Which hadn't happened.

It also would mean the king would want to know for certain who was behind Sim's shooting, unless his steward had the notion he would take the king's place. It was more than likely some relation of the king who wanted the position and had promised Gustafson more money and power than he already had. Same with Lord Comyn.

Alban slashed hard at Gustafson, and was clearly the better swordsman, if for probably no other reason than he practiced at it, had fought in many battles, and generally worked hard for his clan. Gustafson was soft, too busy giving orders and planning assassinations, it seemed.

Every thrust Gustafson made, Alban struck his sword ten times harder. Gustafson swung again, but he didn't have the edge that Alban had. He swung with all his might, but it was half the strength that Alban had, and with every swing Alban made, Gustafson's arm and whole body shook with the impact. Still, he hung onto his sword, kept fighting and not giving up. He knew he had to fight to the death or lose his life when the king was through with him.

Alban wouldn't make it easy on him. The man would pay for his crimes, but he would do it at the king's hand, not his own. Alban struck at Gustafson so hard, he lost his sword. He dove for it, but Alban planted his foot on it and pointed his sword at the steward's throat. "Give it up, Gustafson."

"We will take him," one of Alban's men said.

And he realized two of his guardsmen had arrows trained on Gustafson, but they'd been waiting for him to take down the lord himself.

"Aye, my thanks." Alban only wanted to see to Aila, and as soon as his men took charge of Gustafson, Alban rushed to pull her into his arms. "I love you, Aila, with all my heart." He shouldn't have declared his love for her in front all of his men, but he had to. To tell her how he really felt about her, even if they could do nothing about it.

She was shivering, her lips no longer blue though.

"Let me hand her up to you," one of his men said.

"Aye." Alban mounted his horse, and his guardsman lifted Aila up to him. With her seated across his lap, wrapped securely in his plaid, he said, "I am returning her to the keep. Take Gustafson and Comyn to the king."

"Aye," his men said, one of them handing up her sopping wet chemise, and Alban tucked it in his shirt. Then he rode off to take the lass back to the castle where she could get warm, dry clothes, and dry her hair. Before he could ask her if the men had harmed her in any way, she spoke.

"My sister?"

"She is safe. We found her on the peninsula and Ward will have taken her back to the keep."

"Thank the Lord. What about us?" Her body wasn't shaking as much now, his body warming hers.

There was no *us*, unless Alban stole her away from

all of this. He would have to leave his family, his home. But he realized then he would do just that. Anything to keep her from marrying anyone else.

"How would you feel about leaving all your wealth behind and marrying someone who had no' a coin to his name, no family to speak of, no home, but who loves you dearly and would love you to the end of my days?"

"I wouldna want you to give up everything for me."

"I would do anything for you, Aila. But I dinna know how you would feel about being with me, if you have to give up your properties to do so."

She didn't say anything. Didn't agree that she could do that for him. Was he mistaken about what she truly felt for him? He was a fool to believe she would be willing to give up everything to be with him. Her declaration of love for him had simply been that of a most grateful lady who had found herself in danger of losing her life. Now it was back to reality. For both of them.

What he hadn't expected upon his return was that the king's own guards would arrest *him*!

One of the king's men had taken the lady into the keep, amidst her protests that Alban was innocent of any wrongdoing. He hoped the matter would be cleared up at once and worried that his own brother might be in the dungeon.

When he was taken into the chamber where the king would have audience with his courtiers, Alban saw that Lord Dunlap was in attendance as well. Alban bowed low, then wanted to explain the whole situation, but held his tongue. The king motioned for his guards to leave.

Malcolm sat on his throne looking imperious, his dark brows furrowed. "You knew someone was attempting to kill me and yet you said naught about it to me?"

Lord Dunlap smiled a little.

"The only one I believed might have been involved was Lord Dunlap," Alban said, quite honestly. He wouldn't make the mistake of lying to the king. "But I wasna about to share assumptions when they could turn out to be untrue. What if I were wrong? Then a man could have been condemned for having no part in this. As I investigated further, I discovered the earl had been setup. I didna play into Gustafson's hands as he might have hoped. But I didna know for certain until Sim came forth with real evidence. When Gustafson and Comyn tried to drown Lady Aila and her sister, it was a foregone conclusion. He must no' have been aware my brother and I were looking into the matter also."

"Aye, and had they made another attempt on my life in the meantime?" the king asked darkly.

"Our clansmen were watching out for your safety while Ward and I attempted to learn the truth. We were no' even convinced the hunter who shot Sim had done so by mistake, when he truly meant to hit you. It was possible it was purely an accident. I had no intention of falsely accusing anyone of a crime when there may have been none."

"Yet, you did overhear some bit of conversation where men were talking about killing someone and missing the mark."

"Aye, which was the only reason we thought the hunter had shot Sim. Either on purpose and the shooter didna hit him the first time, or that he was trying to shoot someone else, and Sim got in the way. But we couldna be positive Sim's injury had anything to do with what the men were speaking of."

"When you said we, you mean Lady Aila and you. Correct?"

"Aye, Your Grace."

"Then others must have heard the men's words."

"Nay, my loird."

"You were alone with her?"

Alban suspected the king already knew that. "Aye, Your Grace."

"Why?"

Hell. He had no intention of telling the king about her finding the white stag and chasing it away so the king wouldn't kill it.

"I saw her go off into the woods and worried about her safety."

"Why would she do something like that?"

"She saw a deer, I believe, but it was too young, and she intended to return to the hunt when I came upon her. We heard the men talking after that, and once we felt sure it was safe enough, that they would not see us, we went to join the others. Then she saw the boar, alerted me, and I shouted to everyone who was close enough to hear that the chase was again on. After that, I began looking into who had shot Sim."

"As did Lady Aila and then her sister."

"And my brother and my men, aye. We were trying to learn who had shot Sim, but I forbade Lady Aila to look into the matter."

Alban swore the king was attempting not to smile. Lord Dunlap didn't hide his.

"Because you were trying to protect the lady."

"Aye."

"It seems to me you have shown your loyalty in a way that any king would hope for from his loyal subjects. I wasna sure of your brother's complete allegiance to the crown, but I can see the clan has pledged their trustworthiness in actions, and no' with just a word. In that regard, Lord Comyn's lands are forfeit, and I now have an earldom to offer to you, should you wish to accept my terms."

Shocked to the marrow of his bones, Alban glanced at Lord Dunlap. Ronan and Ward would be just as astounded, he was certain. "Aye, of course, I would be honored, my lord."

"Here is my condition. Lord Dunlap has expressed an interest in the lass, but he assures me you have already stolen her heart—which is neither here nor there as kingdoms are not built on mere love affairs, though they have fallen into ruin over such a thing. Therefore, you will marry the lass. 'Tis your duty after you were so blatantly seeing the lady when you shouldna have been. And at least on one occasion—by your own admission—alone."

Alban tried to keep a straight face in front of the king, to act as solemn in this matter as he thought he should. But he couldn't help himself. He grinned. "Aye, Your Grace. 'Twould be my honor. More than my honor. 'Twould mean the world to me."

Lord Dunlap shook his head, but a glimmer of a smile touched his lips.

"Then it is done. And if you ever suspect someone of making an attempt to take my life again...I hope you would catch him in time...again." Malcolm turned to Lord Dunlap. "I wish a word alone with you now."

"Aye, Your Grace."

And then Alban was released and he bowed to the king and smiled at Lord Dunlap, because he highly suspected the man had something to do with all of this. Men had saved the king's life in the past, but Alban didn't know of any who had come out so well afterwards.

When he walked out of the king's chamber and the guards shut the door, he saw Aila wringing her hands, her eyes bright with tears. Her sister and their maids looked just as anxious. His brother slapped him on the back. "Must be good news or you wouldna be grinning so broadly. Nor would you be leaving the chamber without guards removing you in chains."

"What did he say?" Aila asked Alban, her hands still clenched together.

"That I must wed you." Nothing else mattered. The title or the lands...except as a means to have what he really wanted. Aila.

He wrapped her in his arms and kissed her, ignoring that her sister and their maids were watching. Aila was truly his and the world was right again.

CHAPTER 11

Aila couldn't believe it and was happier than she could remember, except if her parents had been here to witness her marriage to the new Lord of Comyn. To Aila, he would always be Alban, her hero. The Highlander who had protected her so many times, while giving in to his need as a man and kissing her and making her fall in love.

Queen Margaret insisted the wedding take place right away. In three days' time, it was held in the small chapel filled with the guests who had come seeking brides, and those who had been hopeful to find an agreeable lord among them. What pleased Aila, as much as it pleased Alban, his oldest brother, Ronan, had arrived and was just in time for the wedding. He'd teased Alban mercilessly for not only obtaining a lady for a wife, but his own earldom, and jested with Ward just as much for allowing their younger brother to do so when he was the next oldest brother. To which Ward had replied in good humor, "'Tis about time he did something right."

She loved them all, but most of all, she loved Alban. And she was profoundly grateful to Dunlap, for if he hadn't spoken on Alban's behalf, she was certain none of this would have happened.

Lady Umberton seemed genuinely pleased the way things had worked out. Lady Felicia was being Lady Felicia and was trying to make the most of attempting to garner Lord Dunlap's attention further.

Of course, to try and make up for spreading rumors and attempting to get in the new countess's favor, she had given her a gift of a new chemise, one that she'd intended for her own wedding, had it occurred. Aila had to appreciate the gift, no matter how things had begun between them. Though she would never be her friend. Gossips were always gossips and she didn't trust that she wouldn't be the object of the woman's hearsay at some later date.

The festivities proceeded after that, and Aila couldn't believe she was truly married—and to the man she adored. She didn't think the feasting and merrymaking would ever end, but then her sister and their maids and Lady Umberton, and aye, even Lady Felicia, attended her before Alban joined her. She was nervous and excited, and couldn't wait.

***

Alban watched as the ladies took his bride away to the chamber that would be theirs for the night, and then they would be off in the morn straight away so that he could tell Lord Comyn's people he was their new lord and Lady Aila, their countess. She had a country manor and servants of her own, and they would go there when they wished to get away. But for now, he smiled as the ladies all giggled and chatted merrily as they left the great hall to prepare her for him. The thought made his loins tighten.

Lord Dunlap joined Alban in a drink, and said to him, "You saved my life during that first hunt, Alban. Not only that, but you had every intention of proving whether I was guilty or not in the case of attempting to assassinate the king. It would have been easy for you to turn me in for treason. But you didna. A lesser man would have. I wished to repay you."

"My thanks to you, then, Dunlap. To have Lady Aila's hand in marriage was my only hope. And you made it happen. I will be forever in your debt."

"As I am indebted to you. Someday, I will have a wife, and I hope she will adore me the way Aila does you. She is a treasure, but she will surely cause you much vexation."

Alban laughed. "Aye, she is a willful lady. And I look forward to every day I can spend enjoying the time with her. I have a question though, one that I could never seem to find the answer to. Inghean said a servant came for the arrow that was used on Sim. But if Lord Comyn or Gustafson wished to frame you, why did they try to obtain the arrow?"

"I wondered the same thing. Think you the servant would have made a big deal to the healer about the kind of arrow it was for all to hear? 'Look, 'tis a nockless arrow. Who would have used such a weapon on Sim?' Then tongues would have wagged and the accusation would have ended up landing at my feet. As far as I know, I am the only one who uses such an arrow."

"I see your point. And one other thing."

Lord Dunlap cleared his throat. "You dinna suspect I might still be part of the plot, do you?"

Alban smiled. "Nay. Just something I was curious about. When you didna arrive on time to kill the boar your friends Lord Comyn and Lord Tarleton had targeted, what business had you to take care of that was so important?"

Dunlap laughed. "If you must know, I had drunk too much mead when we broke our fast. 'Tis most uncomfortable riding when one needs to relieve oneself. Lady Aila wished to know what my business was too, and had she asked me point blank, I would have told her. But I didna wish to, as I am sure you understand the reason."

"Aye. I thank you again." Alban glanced at the entryway where Ralene was making her way into the great hall. "It seems I have an engagement."

"Off to it then, mon. 'Tis no' done to leave the blushing bride waiting too long."

Alban said good night to him and his brothers and thanked the king for all his generosity and the queen as well. Malcolm's eyes sparkled with amusement and he raised a tankard to him. "Enjoy!"

Alban joined Ralene, and he walked out of the great hall at a quickened pace, but even faster when he headed for the stairs. He ran up them two at a time and finally reached the chamber and knocked.

"'Tis me, your husband." Past ready to make love to his bonny bride.

Alban hurried the ladies out of the chamber, though he was trying not to show his impatience at wanting to be alone with his wife. Would it look like he couldn't wait to ravish her?

It was true, he couldn't wait to make love to his sweet wife. Every time he saw her, got close, felt her warm lips against his, her body hugging his, he'd had a devil of a time getting his raging need for her under control.

As soon as he closed the door, Alban quickly ditched his sword and belt. Aila smiled at him, her red curls cascading over her shoulders, her warm brown eyes alight with excitement. He glanced at her creamy skin and the fine embroidery woven into the chemise's neck and sleeves, but his gaze fastened on her dark nipples pressed against the light fabric and the patch of curly red hair between her legs.

She moved toward him, as he did her, placed her hands on his shoulders, and tilted her head up, expecting a kiss.

He wrapped his arms around her and drew her tightly against him. Her luscious lips parted and he took advantage, kissing her softly at first, then more firmly, and finally tasting her mouth with his tongue, stroking hers, loving her. He dragged his hands through her hair, enjoying the silky feel of the strands while she ran her fingers through his, and her touch made him all the harder.

He burned with a fiery craving to have her, hold her, and join with her as husband and wife. He continued to kiss her deeply, then alternating between soft kisses and harder ones—to which she responded with just as much eagerness. He was trying to remove his brat and still continue to kiss her, not wanting to lose the connection. She pulled away though, grasped his hand, and led him to the bed as if she wanted to have her way with him without removing their clothes. Which was fine with him, if she felt too uncomfortable with being completely naked the first time. His brother had warned him to do whatever the lass wished, as if his brother had to advise him on such a matter!

Instead of climbing into bed, she made him sit down first, and then she crouched at his feet and pulled off his shoes and stockings. She seemed unsure what to do next, so he stood, and skimmed his fingers over her breasts, making her nipples tighten with need, and then he leaned down, and while he fondled one breast, he took the other partially in his mouth and suckled through the sheer fabric. She moaned, her heart already beating wildly in her breast, nearly as wildly as his own.

Yet he felt a tenderness for her that he'd never felt

for any other woman, and a desire for her that could not be quenched. He slid the chemise over her shoulders and it dropped only to settle on her hips. Her breasts were a nice size, perfect for caressing and kissing and suckling.

When she pulled his shirt off his shoulders, it fell straight to the rushes on the floor. For a moment, she took in her fill of him, her mouth curving in a wicked smile.

His cock stirred with eagerness, and he pulled her chemise down her hips, and let it drop to the floor. Then he lifted her, turned, and placed her on the bed. There were no words, just more kissing and touching, her hands in his hair as he moved in beside her and began to caress her breast. Her breathing was growing as ragged as his as he moved his hand lower, sweeping down her belly, and then he began to caress that place that made her writhe to his touch. Moan with pleasure. Encourage him to press harder. And then he plunged a finger into her sweet chasm. Stroking her and kissing her at the same time. Loving the sweet and musky scent of her. Her softness and curves. Her eagerness and desire.

She practically held her breath, and then she let out a cry, muffled by his kiss. He spread her legs and centered himself, pushing slightly to let her get used to the pressure, pushed in to take her virginity, then paused to let her breathe through the pain.

But she reached out to pull him closer, letting him know she was ready. Eager to have her fully, he pressed forward, entering her deeper, until he was all the way in, and began to thrust. He wouldn't prolong this for her, not until she was healed from their first time. Not that he could last long anyway as much as she had stirred his loins tonight and every other night he'd thought about her.

And then he came, spilling his seed in her, loving the lady who was his wife through nothing short of a miracle.

***

Aila loved her Highlander, loved the way he was holding back, wanting to please her, but his face had shown the strain in his restraint. She couldn't have been happier to be with him, though she had no idea what the morrow would bring.

How would Lord Comyn's people feel about their new lord? Ward and Ronan said they would bring their guards to help ensure the transition was without trouble, though Alban had the king's backing in this, so she suspected some might grumble, but would learn to live with the new rule.

Would they accept her as the new lady of the manor? She would not worry about it. As far as she was concerned, she and Alban could manage anything, making their new life together, and showing their people they had nothing to worry about.

She would miss her sister most of all. But Wynda assured her she would see her soon, once everything was settled. The queen wished for Wynda to stay so that she could still find a husband among the visiting lords.

Mai, her lady's maid, would go with her, while

Raleen stayed with Wynda. Mai had run to fetch water for Aila so she could wash up quickly before they broke their fast. They planned to leave early that morn. Her maid cry out in the corridor, and then begin to scold someone. Aila hurried to the chamber door to see what had happened and opened it.

Red-faced, Sim was trying to wipe Mai's gown off with the sleeve of his shirt, which had her maid blushing furiously and grabbing his hand to make him stop.

"My lady," Sim quickly said, dropping into a bow. "The king wished me to inform the earl that I will be coming with you. I was in too much of a hurry and ran into the maid, I dare say, and apologize profusely." He was as wet as her maid, and all Aila could do was laugh.

Until she recalled that Sim had some affection for the healer's assistant and so there would be no blossoming romance between her maid and him.

"And the lass you were going to wed?"

"Oh." He looked down at the floor. "She has already set her eyes upon some other lad."

Aila smiled. "Well, then, Sim, I will pass the word along to the earl. And no harm done." Except that her maid was thoroughly embarrassed. "Why dinna you change into something dry in our old chamber, Mai, and I will get the water."

"Nay, 'tis my duty," Sim said, and offered to take the pitcher from her maid.

Mai glanced at Aila to see if it was all right.

"Thank you, Sim," Aila said and she couldn't help

but think back to the way she had met Alban. One pitcher of water between them. And then later a kiss. Which had sealed their fate from the beginning.

Suddenly, Alban was joining her, his arm settling around her shoulders. "This reminds me of something that happened to me a while back."

Mai and Sim waited to hear what the earl was referring to.

Aila took Alban's hand and led him straight back into the chamber and shut the door. "We dinna need for everyone to know."

And then they were kissing again, as the newly married were known to do. As long as they could be quick about it, they were eager to make love one more time before their long journey, as if that were the last time they might ever do so.

Which was not the case, she realized, as he made love to her in their tent at night, all the way across Scotland, and she couldn't have cherished him any more than she did.

Then when they had eaten their meal for the night and were about to retire to their tent, they saw the white stag, as if it were leading them on their new adventure. Alban wrapped his arms around Aila and kissed her cheek, her back snuggled next to his chest as they stood watching the stag. The hart finally dipped his head a little and moved off into the woods.

Alban and Aila knew the stag was a sign of only good things to come.

Alban never believed he'd be so lucky when he went to the king's festivities, disgruntled and hoping to stay with his men out in the glen. That all changed when he ran into Aila in the castle that first day, and couldn't stop thinking about her after that. She had turned his world inside out in the best way possible.

Despite the long road ahead of them, settling into their new castle and being comfortable with the people there, he knew with Aila at his side, he could conquer any trouble, no matter how difficult. But until then, he concentrated on making the journey as comfortable for Aila as he could, though his brothers teased him about how in the past he would always push forward no matter the hour. And now he couldn't wait to stop for the night to join his lovely bride. Which had his wife saying they could continue their journey, if they were delaying it too much. And Alban giving his brothers his battle-stern look that told them to say not another word, and them laughing as brothers are inclined to do.

ABOUT THE AUTHOR

Bestselling and award-winning author **Terry Spear** has written over fifty paranormal romance novels and four medieval Highland historical romances. Her first werewolf romance, *Heart of the Wolf,* was named a 2008 *Publishers Weekly*'s Best Book of the Year, and her subsequent titles have garnered high praise and hit the *USA Today* bestseller list. A retired officer of the U.S. Army Reserves, Terry lives in Crawford, Texas, where she is working on her next werewolf romance, continuing her new series about shapeshifting jaguars, and cougars, having fun with her young adult novels, and playing with her two Havanese puppies, Max and Tanner. For more information, please visit www.terryspear.com, or follow her on Twitter, @TerrySpear. She is also on Facebook at http://www.facebook.com/terry.spear. And on Wordpress at:

Terry Spear's Shifters
http://terryspear.wordpress.com

ALSO BY TERRY SPEAR

Heart of the Cougar Series: Cougar's Mate, Book

Call of the Cougar, Book 2

Taming the Wild Cougar, Book 3

Covert Cougar Christmas (Novella)

Double Cougar Trouble, Book 4

* * *

Heart of the Bear Series

Loving the White Bear, Book 1

* * *

The Highlanders Series: Winning the Highlander's

Heart, The Accidental Highland Hero, Highland Rake, Taming the Wild Highlander, The Highlander, Her Highland Hero, The Viking's Highland Lass, His Wild Highland Lass (Novella), Vexing the Highlander (Novella)

Other historical romances: Lady Caroline & the Egotistical Earl, A Ghost of a Chance at Love

* * *

Heart of the Wolf Series: Heart of the Wolf, Destiny of the Wolf, To Tempt the Wolf, Legend of the White Wolf, Seduced by the Wolf, Wolf Fever, Heart of the Highland Wolf, Dreaming of the Wolf, A SEAL in Wolf's Clothing, A Howl for a Highlander, A Highland Werewolf Wedding, A SEAL Wolf Christmas, Silence of the Wolf, Hero of a Highland Wolf, A Highland Wolf Christmas, A SEAL Wolf Hunting; A Silver Wolf Christmas, A SEAL Wolf in Too Deep, Alpha Wolf Need Not Apply, Billionaire in Wolf's Clothing, Between a Rock and a Hard Place (2017), White Wolf Christmas (2017), SEAL Wolf Undercover (2017)

SEAL Wolves: To Tempt the Wolf, A SEAL in Wolf's Clothing, A SEAL Wolf Christmas, A SEAL Wolf Hunting, A SEAL Wolf in Too Deep, SEAL Wolf

Undercover (2017)

Silver Bros Wolves: Destiny of the Wolf, Wolf Fever, Dreaming of the Wolf, Silence of the Wolf, A Silver Wolf Christmas, Alpha Wolf Need Not Apply, Between a Rock and a Hard Place (2017)

White Wolves: Legend of the White Wolf, Dreaming of a White Wolf Christmas (2017)

Billionaire Wolves: Billionaire in Wolf's Clothing, Billionaire Wolf Christmas (2018)

Highland Wolves: Heart of the Highland Wolf, A Howl for a Highlander, A Highland Werewolf Wedding, Hero of a Highland Wolf, A Highland Wolf Christmas

* * *

Heart of the Jaguar Series: Savage Hunger, Jaguar Fever, Jaguar Hunt, Jaguar Pride, A Very Jaguar Christmas

* * *

Romantic Suspense: Deadly Fortunes, In the Dead of the Night, Relative Danger, Bound by Danger

* * *

Vampire romances: Killing the Bloodlust, Deadly Liaisons, Huntress for Hire, Forbidden Love

Vampire Novellas: Vampiric Calling, Siren's Lure, Seducing the Huntress

* * *

Futuristic/Science Fiction Romance: Galaxy Warrior

Other Romance: Exchanging Grooms, Marriage, Las Vegas Style

* * *

Teen/Young Adult/Fantasy Books

The World of Fae:

The Dark Fae, Book 1

The Deadly Fae, Book 2

The Winged Fae, Book 3

The Ancient Fae, Book 4

Dragon Fae, Book 5

Hawk Fae, Book 6

Phantom Fae, Book 7

Golden Fae, Book 8

Phantom Fae, Book 9

Falcon Fae (TBA)

The World of Elf:

The Shadow Elf

The Darkland Elf (TBA)

Blood Moon Series:

Kiss of the Vampire

The Vampire...In My Dreams

Demon Guardian Series:

The Trouble with Demons

Demon Trouble, Too

Demon Hunter (TBA)

Non-Series for Now:

Ghostly Liaisons

The Beast Within

Courtly Masquerade

Deidre's Secret

The Magic of Inherian:

The Scepter of Salvation

The Mage of Monrovia

Emerald Isle of Mists (TBA)

EXCERPT FROM:

WINNING THE HIGHLANDER'S HEART

TERRY SPEAR

Winning the Highlander's Heart

Published by

Vinspire, Inc.

Copyright © 2010 by Terry Spear

Discover more about Terry Spear at:

http://www.terryspear.com/

CHAPTER ONE

WEST SUSSEX, REIGN OF HENRY I

"My lady!"

The Countess of Brecken's lady-in-waiting, Mai, threw the door open to Anice's guest chambers at Arundel Castle, then quickly slammed it shut. Two gray curls fell loose from the older woman's plaited hair; her ivory cheeks flushed. She breathed in rapid, shortened breaths, and her gray eyes were rounder than the full moon. "His Grace is headed this way. Lady Anice, ye must hide."

'Twas folly for Anice to think she could avoid the king's unwanted solicitations for long. And she, his wife's cousin.

"I am no' hiding, Mai," Anice scolded, "like I said before. I am making myself unavailable to his...charms."

She tied the rope to the bed leg, then ran to the nearest window and tossed the other end out. If the English ladies of her cousin's court had not treated her with contempt because of her Scottish heritage, she would be visiting with the queen right now and could save herself the trouble of fleeing from the king's attempted seduction, again.

"Och, my lady, you cannot mean to—"

"Aye, Mai, I mean to. Just delay His Grace if he should come knocking at the door before I have vanished. Moreover, for heaven's sakes be sure to hide the rope. Tell him I am with Her Grace sewing in her solar."

Anice lifted the full skirt of her bliaut and chemise underneath, and scrambled atop the embroidered cushion resting on the stone window seat.

With heart pounding, she peered below. 'Twas a shame it opened on the inner bailey of Arundel Castle where women washed garments in large wooden barrels, the blacksmith pounded on an anvil, sending sparks flying, and beyond, noblemen's sons thrust and parried wooden swords on the warm summer day. Still, with everyone a goodly distance across the bailey from where she attempted escape and very much preoccupied, mayhap no one would notice a lady slipping down a rope from the second story window.

Mai wrung her hands. "My lady, what if ye should fall?"

"You are not helping me, Mai. Hush. I have done this many times before as a wee lass. You know that."

But this time was entirely different from her many escapades of the past. 'Twas difficult enough to find a husband who would live long enough to give her wedded bliss, but she was not about to be tupped by a lusty king who already had a wife.

Anice tugged on the rope and when it held, she climbed onto the stone sill. Grasping the rope, she swung over the edge and held on tight. Her arms strained while she wrapped her legs around the rope and began to shimmy down.

A pounding on her chamber door produced a rash of chill bumps to trail along her arms.

Across the courtyard, a man shouted, "My lady!"

A streak of panic shot into her bones as she clambered down the rope.

Couldn't a lady take a walk in the kitchen gardens—even if she got there by extraordinary means—without causing an uproar in the king's staff?

The thud of hooves galloped on the grassy earth in her direction. She cursed under her breath. She needed no horseman's help to descend a rope. Her hands slipped on the coarse hemp and her heartbeat quickened. She was a wee bit out of practice.

"Drop to me! I'll catch you!" the man's deep,

sexy voice shouted with a distinctive Scottish burr, as he guided his horse beneath her.

She gave a lady-like snort. If she dropped to whoever was below her, no doubt her skirts would fly up around her ears. "'Tis nay concern of yours. Move away." She meant to speak her words harshly, commanding the man to do her bidding at once, but her voice sounded way too soft and overmuch like pleading to her ears.

She glanced down at him, sitting astride his roan destrier. Belted at the waist, a pleated saffron wool tunic rose to mid-thigh, exposing his brawny muscular legs. The narrow tunic sleeves stretched down his arms, widening at the wrist, revealing large hands that clutched his horse's reins with a fierce grip.

Her gaze drew up his massive chest to his dark brown hair, highlighted with reddish strands hanging loose about his broad shoulders, framing and at the same time softening the harsh angles of his face. He had the kind of manly nose that befit Scottish royalty, a sturdy square chin that tilted up toward the heavens, and the kind of lips women begged to kiss. Not a Norman or a Saxon, but a handsome devil of a Highlander. 'Twas not his broad shoulders and chest that gave her pause, but his furrowed brow and darkened brown eyes that compelled a longer look.

Her fingers slid again and her heart leapt into her throat. To her surprise, the man quickly stood in his stirrups, his hands outstretched ready to catch her.

"Jump, lass, and I shall catch ye."

A sprinkle of perspiration trickled between her breasts. 'Twas not too far to fall, only one more story now. If she landed on the gentleman, he'd no doubt break her tumble nicely. She continued to slide down the rope, her arms quickly wearying. At twenty summers, she was getting much too old for this.

The rough rope tore at her tender flesh. Her fingers burned. Trying to ignore the pain, she clenched her teeth, and lowered herself further.

"My lady!" The man grabbed at her.

When he caught her foot, she nearly fell and gasped in surprise. She kicked his hand away. "I do no' need your help." Not unless the hand belonged to a Highland laird who wished to take her away from here and back to her home without delay.

His hands slid up her hose-covered leg and rose to her naked thigh. She screamed out in shock. What in heaven's name were his hands doing up her chemise?

"Sorry, if you would quit your squirming—"

"You are no' a gentleman," she snapped, and let go of the rope before the rider manhandled her much more, landing squarely in his lap. He groaned as if she'd caused him pain. Here she thought he looked strong enough to wage the toughest battles without concern.

His large, capable hands curved around her waist with a possessiveness she should be resenting, though she couldn't help wish he'd carry her away home again, and free her from the king's advances. The Highlander smelled of horse, leather, and man—incredibly intriguing—but way too close for comfort, yet she breathed him in like it was the last breath she would ever take. Huskily, he retorted next to her ear, "And ye, lass, are no' a—"

Before he could utter another word, she hopped from his horse, catching the hem of her bliaut on his stirrup. Mortified, she nearly ripped the fabric to get it loose. How many courtiers watched her antics now? She worked on her gown, too busy to find out. Perspiration freckled her brow and her skin grew as hot as the armorer's fire.

"If you would allow me, lass, to free it, you would not show off your chemise or other more remarkable qualities." He grinned broadly and tugged to release her hem. His dark brown eyes now nearly black smiled back at her. Dimples punctuated his bronzed cheeks, but it was the raw look of lust that shook her to the core.

Humiliated, she jerked her gown loose and landed unceremoniously on her bottom on the grassy ground. Horror of horrors her gowns were hiked to her knees. She yanked the hem down with a scowl. His heated gaze shifted from her legs to her eyes and again, his lips curved up at the corners.

Bolting from the ground, she wished she could disappear like a dewdrop evaporated on a sunny day. She darted around the backside of the circular keep. Concerned about who might have watched her jester-like antics, she avoided looking altogether.

Her breath quickened and heart beat as fast as if she'd run a mile through the heather in the middle of summer. Only 'twas not her run that sent her heart soaring, but the man's heated hands that had touched her naked skin and his roguish smile that burned her through and through.

Gently rubbing her hands together, she attempted to soften the sting. 'Twas not the way she planned to spend her days at Arundel. Somehow, she had to convince her cousin to speak with the king on her behalf and allow her to return home before things got out of hand. Well, more so than they were already.

The whole court was sure to know of her escapade by the time she broke her fast.

Reaching the side of the motte that faced the River Arun, she spied Queen Matilda seated upon a stone bench surrounded by her ladies-in-waiting. 'Twas not good.

If Mai told the king Anice was visiting with her cousin in her chambers, he'd know she lied. Mayhap not. He might have no idea where his wife sat at the moment. Then again, Anice was certain he'd be apprised of her window escape now, too. Would he have a good laugh? Or be angry with her?

She lifted her chin in obstinacy. She refused to be one of his mistresses.

"Lady Anice," Matilda called out near the corner of the garden, enjoying a bit of sun on the warm day.

"Your Grace," Anice curtsied and hurried to join her. "May I have a word with my lady alone?"

The queen's hair, like her ladies', hung in long plaits free of the veils she had hated to wear when she lived with the Black Nuns of Romsey. Even now, Anice could envision Matilda yanking off her veil and stomping on it in defiance of her Aunt Christina who was abbess, and the subsequent beating and scolding she'd received from her. The words Matilda had spoken in her defense before the Archbishop of

Anselm of Canterbury before she was allowed to marry King Henry echoed in Anice's mind. Matilda had not taken the holy vows, and her Aunt Christina had veiled her to keep her from the lust of the Normans. She'd been much sought after as a bride, having turned down both William de Warenne, 2nd Earl of Surrey and Alan Rufus, Lord of Richmond. 'Twas rumored even Henry's older brother, William Rufus, king until his untimely death during the hunting accident, considered marrying her. Despite Henry's other more recent love interests, he had espoused he'd been long attached to Matilda, and had long adored her character.

Now, colorful silken cases elongated Matilda's tresses while metal tassels extended them even further. 'Twas every lady's desire to have the thickest, longest hair. Yet, Anice still hid hers under a veil and wimple. Teased mercilessly by the other ladies about her wild red hair and fiery temper, she chose to keep her tresses hidden until she returned to Brecken Castle.

Her cousin tilted her chin down, her eyes worried. "What ails you, Anice? Your cheeks are as red as Elizabeth's gown."

'Twas the man's hands that had clutched Anice's bare thigh that forced the blush in her cheeks. Not to mention exposing her legs and...och, she wouldn't be able to forget the look on the Highlander's face—a scoundrel's fascination and unbridled amusement—all at her expense.

But the queen wouldn't want to hear about that. Nor that the king had propositioned Anice thrice already. He would populate the English countryside with the greatest number of illegitimate children of any of their kings, if he had his way.

"Please, you must speak to His Grace and convince him I need return to my people, Your Grace."

Matilda motioned for her ladies to leave them. Her ladies quit the garden, standing out of their hearing, but waiting still to serve her. Matilda spoke softly. "You know His Grace wishes you to marry a Norman gentleman."

"*I dinna* want that!" Anice scowled. "You were born in Fifeshire yourself, Your Grace. You were..."

Anice fell silent. She wanted to remind her cousin that to an extent Matilda had been forced to marry to make an alliance of sorts to quell the unrest along the Scottish border. Not only that, but to tie the Norman bloodline into the queen's royal Saxon line. Though they were cousins, Anice still had to choose her words carefully.

"What is wrong, Anice?" Her cousin's words were spoken calmly, but she appeared more than concerned.

Your husband tried to interest me in joining him in his chamber earlier this morn while you were at chapel. That's what Anice wanted to tell her, but she could not. She knew very well Henry's philandering hurt Matilda more than she would admit, but the queen would not show how much Henry upset her and Anice would not reveal she was his latest target, if she could avoid it.

Anice bit her lip. How could she convince Matilda she must leave Arundel without telling her of the king's amorous advances? Did the man not stock enough fillies in his stable already? She blew out her breath. "'Tis naught, Your Grace. I am only homesick."

She knew Matilda wanted to return to Westminster where she mainly held court, though like now, she often accompanied Henry on his travels across England, but she hoped her cousin would understand her need to return home.

Wordlessly Matilda studied her, and Anice wondered if her cousin knew the truth of her distress.

Taking a deep, exasperated breath, Anice considered her dilemma. She wished no part of any Norman laird the king wanted her to marry either, who would wed her for her properties and not care one whit about a woman whose Scottish heritage they scorned. Yet, another concern plagued her. Would any marriage she attempted be truly cursed? She squashed the worrisome notion down into the pit of her stomach. For now, avoiding the king proved tantamount.

Not only that, the most dreadful feeling something awful would befall her people at Brecken Castle continued to plague her. Early on, she'd learned to hide from others these strange premonitions that oft came true, but she couldn't contain the dark foreboding that filled her with dread now, forcing her to seek any means necessary to return home where she might do some good.

How could she leave Arundel without the king's permission? She could not. Not unless her cousin convinced him to allow Anice to return home.

Squinting to get a better look at the inner bailey, she watched as the man—who'd touched her so inappropriately—rode toward the stables with three others. His broad shoulders and the way he held himself erect commanded respect. Impressive. He wore a claymore at his back and a dagger at his hip. And his clothes were of quality fabric. He rode a nobleman's horse, not a common mount, so she assumed he was a man of some import.

"Who is that?" Anice enquired.

"Earl of Pembrinton, but you would do well to avoid the man."

Anice raised a brow, genuinely intrigued. "Why?"

"He seeks audience with His Grace as he is in search of an English bride. It matters not whether she is young and pretty, or that he loves her. He desires what most men crave. Power and money. He is a titled lord without properties."

Anice's heart fluttered. "Mayhap I should meet this Highlander." Though she had already met him, *way* too intimately. But perhaps he would agree to return her home, *if* she could obtain the king's permission.

Matilda shook her head quickly. "He is not for you, cousin. From what I have heard, he had some difficulty with a couple of Scottish families and marriage alliances. Marrying an English woman would end the strife."

Anice's blood heated like a blade of steel grew white hot over an open flame. To think he would prefer an Englishwoman to a bonnie Scottish lass. "But if he seeks property and—"

"I am certain he also believes marrying an English lady will afford him greater...entitlements."

"Then he is nay a true Highlander, but a...a blackguard."

"Watch what you say, Anice. I know how strongly you feel about the English, but I am married to His Grace and this is my rightful place now." She took a deep steadying breath. "Not only that, but the English educated King Malcolm, after all. My father loved my mother, though he was a Scotsman and she, a Wessex-born princess. Now Prince David has taken a fancy to a Norman lady here, while receiving his education with us. I am sure if King Henry is agreeable, my brother will marry her. 'Tis just the way of things."

Anice groaned deep inside.

The Scottish kings were bought and paid for by the English. Even Matilda's brother, King Alexander, was considering taking King Henry's illegitimate daughter, Sybilla, for his wife. *That* was why her cousin Alexander, had given her to King Henry as his ward, rather than her being a ward of the Scottish king when her uncle died so suddenly.

Exasperated, Anice sighed deeply.

Matilda patted her arm. "Marry whom His Grace presents to you. You will learn to embrace the changes as I have done. Marriages are partnerships after all. Marrying for love...well, you will grow to love whomever you wed. As for Lord

McNeill, 'tis folly to think you will change his mind about an English bride. Let him well enough alone, dear cousin."

Anice curtseyed to Matilda as her cousin motioned for her ladies to return to her.

But Anice would not be thwarted. If the Highlander needed a bride and she needed a husband, the match seemed perfect. Well, almost. Mayhap she would not like his temperament so very much. Though the notion he would touch more than her naked thigh with his large, gentle hands certainly appealed. What would they feel like holding her close? And what would it be like to kiss those smiling lips of his? There was only one way to find out.

With her heart beating hard, she hastened for the keep where the Highlanders had disappeared. She entered the great hall and ignored the roving eyes of two English knights who glanced her way.

Then she spied the great man and his equally large companions. Her heart skittered.

Laird MacNeill stood betwixt the other two, taller by an inch or so, his hair a richer brown, his eyes the same earthy dark color. The fourth man, a blond with a beard, was nowhere in sight. She turned her attention back to Laird MacNeill. A sensuous smile curved his mouth, forming dimples in his cheeks. But his gaze wasn't focused on her. Instead, he eyed another lady, an *English* lady, standing near the entrance to the hall. The woman's dark tresses were plaited down her front, but her hair wasn't half as thick or long as Anice's. Inwardly Anice smiled at the thought, but on the other hand, she wanted sorely to scream at the Highlander who made a fool of himself over the Englishwoman.

Rogue.

The other two Highlanders were fairer, their long hair fastened back. She folded her arms. Mayhap if Laird MacNeill were not interested in her, one of the other gentlemen would be.

As if the youngest one had heard her thoughts, he turned and smiled at her. Well built despite his youth, his hair was the lightest brown of the three men, and a slight scar marred his otherwise smooth cheek. Before she could consider the other gentleman, the youngest quirked a brow to see her gawking at him. Instantly, her cheeks heated. She quickly unfolded her arms and smoothed down her wool gown. The slightest of smiles curved the corners of his mouth, then he tugged on Laird MacNeill's sleeve.

In no way did she act appropriately. She had neither her lady-in-waiting nor a maid attending her, nor was anyone nearby with proper authority, who could formerly introduce her to these gentlemen. Yet, she remained rooted to the stone floor like an oak, unwilling to yield while she contemplated how to approach the Highlanders.

They seemed as reluctant to breech protocol and stood their ground, though they commented freely to one another, smiling with undisguised admiration while she stood ogling them impolitely.

She lowered her lashes and considered the rushes littering the floor. Mayhap this wasn't a good idea after all. Would they think her a brazen woman to...to wish to make their acquaintance in such a fashion? Aye, they would imagine her nothing but a common leman.

Then, too, what did they think of her actions when she'd climbed out the window?

She wrung her hands suddenly conscious they were cold and clammy. Then she turned, intent on taking a walk...anywhere but here where she was making a fool of herself.

Anice hoped the Highlanders, well one of them at least, would follow her outside so that she could convince him to speak to the king on her behalf and solicit his agreement to return her home. But she heard no footsteps echoing her own and knew then her folly. She was dressed as a lady in exquisite garments, the blue wool the finest of cloth. So they would not think her a serving girl. But these men wanted more than just power and money, or at least the tallest of the three...Laird MacNeill did.

He wanted a lady of quality, but she had to be an English lady.

And that, Anice would never be.

She stomped down the path to the herbal and vegetable garden outside of the kitchen. Hedge walls surrounded the rectangular outdoor room. In seclusion, she walked along the stone walkways, each separating sections of the garden for easier cutting of the plants for meals, medicine, and other uses. Lavender scented the air in the sweetest floral fragrance. She nearly forgot her annoyance when she breathed in the heady smell. But when she continued along the stone path, she fumed about the Highlander again.

Laird MacNeill had a Scottish accent like her. Why should he not like hearing the sound of his countrymen's burr? 'Twas not so bad a sound to her ear.

Footsteps reverberated behind her, and she whipped around, not sure what to expect. Hoping to find the handsome laird following her. Wishing he'd ask her name and want her, just like she wanted him...well, any Highlander to take her away from all this...to return her to her own lands where she'd take on the role of lady of Brecken Castle.

What she found made her heart sink like a stone thrown into the loch. The cook curtseyed to her, then reached down and snipped basil, chive, and red valerian for the meal.

Mayhap, Anice had to find some other Highlander laird if not one of the three were brave enough to attempt to seek audience with her. These did not impress her well enough.

She greeted the cook, then stalked out of the gardens and across the courtyard. She would find some other knights to take her home.

***

Malcolm MacNeill and his youngest brother, Angus, watched the defiant young woman stride toward the stables, while their brother, Dougald, remained behind in the keep trying to find out who she was. Her bearing and dress were impeccable and of the finest fabrics. Definitely a lady. Though he'd never seen one climb out a castle window before to escape from...well, he wasn't sure from what and he still intended to find out.

The interest she'd shown in them just now in the great hall...

Malcolm smiled. He could tell she was intrigued with him by the way her cheeks colored so beautifully and her perky breasts lifted when her heartbeat quickened. Her green eyes had darkened, just enough to fascinate him further. Had she wanted him to run his hands over more than just her naked thigh?

He sighed deeply. 'Twas an English lady he was bound to wed. Yet, the lass captivated him like no other. But having an English wife...well, he knew he and his brothers would be more accepted by the king and other nobles if Malcolm and his kin married English ladies. Besides, after the trouble he'd had with Brenna, then Catherine...

He shook his head. No more fiery-tempered Scottish lasses.

Was she here looking for a husband like so many of the ladies on the queen's staff? At least he assumed she was on the queen's coterie. More importantly, did the lass hold properties? Or was she like him? Having title, but no land? He had no need of a beautiful, young, titled, and penniless woman. He could offer her nothing in return. Then he chided himself. She was Scottish.

Serving as a steward for his older brother, James, had satisfied him for a while, but now, it was time to settle down. To have lands to call his own. That would remain his sole focus for the time being, he reminded himself.

Malcolm crossed his arms. "What is taking

Dougald so long?"

Angus shook his head. "I imagine he is still trying to discover who the young woman is." He glanced at Malcolm. "Think you she is the one for you?"

"She appeared interested, but she is Scottish."

"Mayhap she is already betrothed anyway." Angus drew taller. "Mayhap she was only interested in seeing Highland warriors up close."

Malcolm smiled. "Aye."

"She is a bonny lass. If you dinna please her, mayhap I might have a go."

"She pleases *me*. I do not know about the other way around." Malcolm studied the wiggle of her narrow hips as her blue gown flowed over her backside. Soft curves and all woman. Touching every part of her came to mind, her full pouty lips, her nervous hands, the swell of her fine breasts, and more of her satiny, naked thighs. "She pleases me."

Dougald stepped outside to join them.

"Well?" Malcolm asked, but seeing the look on his brother's stern face, knew he'd found out nothing. "You did not find out anything."

"Nay, but we have an audience with the king."

"I want to know about that woman," Malcolm nodded in the direction of the lady, who was arguing vehemently with some well-dressed gentleman. Malcolm squinted in an attempt to recognize the man. Ah, the marshal in charge of the stables. Twice she wiggled her finger at the marshal to punctuate her statement, though Malcolm stood too far away to hear her words.

Dougald chuckled. "She appears to be a handful." His brother should know, as much as he'd always gotten caught up with that kind of wench in the past, Malcolm thought.

The woman turned and stormed back toward the castle, but as soon as she caught sight of the MacNeill brothers watching her, she stopped dead as if she'd reached the edge of a cliff and stood in peril of falling to her death.

Malcolm's gaze dropped to her bodice, snuggly fitting her breasts, the newer form of gown meant to show off ladies' curves rather than hide them. A girdle of pale blue silk rope wound above her waist, crossed behind, then knotted in front with metal tassels hanging down from them. Certainly for this lady, the girdle accentuated all of the right curves. His attention switched to her hair hidden beneath white cloth. Why, when all the other ladies of the queen's staff showed off their lovely tresses, did this lady not wear her hair unveiled?

"Either she is afraid of us," Angus remarked, placing his hands on his hips, "or she is interested in us, as you have said."

For a moment, she wrung her hands as her gaze focused on Malcolm's, then she strode straight toward them. Rather, toward the entrance to the keep. Her cheeks were positively cherry, and a wisp of hair the color of spun gold, tinted red, fluttered loose from her wimple. Though there were no freckles to bridge her nose, Malcolm thought she resembled a distant cousin on his mother's side. He curbed the notion that twisted his insides. She wasn't a relative certainly, but she was Scottish.

'Twas the end of any interest he had in the vixen. He breathed deeply, trying to rein in his feelings for the woman. He reminded himself any woman he'd touched so intimately would have the same effect on him. Even now, his shaft sprang to life when the image came to mind of spreading her silky thighs, and burying himself deep inside her. He'd not been with a woman in far too long.

She tilted her chin even higher and avoided looking at them when she stormed past. Though he caught the look of her eyes as green as the sea and angry as if whipped into a frenzy on a stormy day. Just like his cousins would be when he and his brothers riled her. He twisted his mouth in annoyance. The woman could intrigue him all she wanted, but he could have no part of her.

He shook his head, wondering how he could have left his native land only to end up in the English castle, lusting after a Scottish lady.

Once she disappeared within the keep, Dougald said, "You dinna think she is Scottish, do you?"

Malcolm ground his teeth in silence and nodded. "Aye, that she is."

His little brother laughed. "Here, Malcolm has convinced each of us to select an English bride and what are we losing our heads over? A Scottish lass?"

"Think you she is here," Dougald asked, ever the man of reason, "looking for an English laird to be her husband?

"Mayhap." Malcolm attempted to appear as though the thought didn't disconcert him, but it did, though why the devil he should care shook him up. Finding a wife to wed was a matter of necessity. 'Twas time to put his title to use, granted to him for having saved King Henry's brother's life, Robert Curthose, during the Crusades. 'Twas time to have a castle, lands, his own people to command, and a bairn to leave his title to. Too bad he had to suffer a wife to make it happen. "If the lady is the king's ward, he may be considering a suitable contract for her hand in marriage."

"Possibly she thought we were some of her kinsmen, then finding we were not, she quickly dismissed that notion," Dougald said, rubbing his two-day growth of beard.

"You have a good point." Malcolm motioned to the keep. "Come, we shall see the king." Though he had to take care of more important business, his thoughts shifted to the feel of the woman's naked skin in his grasp and the sight of her curvaceous legs when she fell on her arse on the grassy ground, her gown resting at her knees, exposing her for his pleasure. Instantly, the blood rushed to his groin again. A bonny lass indeed and one to stay well away from. The rope-climbing incident from the keep tower should have warned him he'd do well to avoid her.

He glanced back at the gate. Had she been trying to leave the castle grounds without escort? Why in heaven's name would she attempt such a dangerous thing?

He shook his head and hastened into the keep, intent on finding out everything he could about the lass...but only for curiosity sake. 'Twas for no other reason he wished to concern himself with the lass. Not because he couldn't shake the vision of her cat-like eyes that held him in contempt, nor the way her cheeks burned with embarrassment, nor the passionate manner in which she expressed herself with the marshal. 'Twas not because he felt obligated from rescuing her from the tower, nor because the feel of her silky skin sent a pleasure-seeking desire coursing through his body.

Simply curiosity overwhelmed him and he had to investigate her further to satisfy this need. 'Twas no other reason for his interest in her.

"Malcolm," Dougald whispered to him. "You are headed the wrong way. What are you thinking about that has you headed in the direction of the ladies' chambers?"

Thanks so much for reading the excerpt for *Winning the Highlander's Heart.*

The novellas, *His Highland Lass* and *Vexing the Highlander*, are prequels, stories that occurred before *Winning the Highlander's Heart* in The Highlander's series. I have eight full length novels available in the series now.

Have fun loving the Highlanders!

Terry Spear